Not for
a Billion
Gazillion
Dollars

Not for a Billion Gazillion Dollars

PAULA DANZIGER

Delacorte Press

Published by
Delacorte Press
Bantam Doubleday Dell Publishing Group, Inc.
666 Fifth Avenue
New York, New York 10103

Library of Congress Cataloging in Publication Data
Danziger, Paula, [date of birth]
    Not for a billion gazillion dollars / Paula Danziger.
        p.   cm.
    Summary: Eleven-year-old Matthew, trying desperately to earn
enough to buy a coveted computer program, learns the importance of
money and eventually starts his own business. Sequel to "Earth to
Matthew."
    ISBN 0-385-30819-1
    [1. Moneymaking projects—Fiction. 2. Money—Fiction.]
    I. Title.
PZ7.D2394No   1992
[Fic]—dc20   92-2735
                                                          CIP
                                                          AC

Manufactured in the United States of America

October 1992

10 9 8 7 6 5 4 3 2 1

BVG

Acknowledgments

TO KEVIN DAVIS,
a truly great teacher and an even better friend

And many thanks:
to my friends who listened to much of this manuscript on the phone—Bruce Coville, Pam Swallow—and to Ben Blair, kid consultant, and to Craig Virden, for being a very wonderful editor.

Chapter 1

"What do you think, Matthew, that money just grows on trees?" Mrs. Martin stares at her son.

Matthew, who is on his knees with his hands in a praying position, debates saying to his mother, *If money doesn't grow on trees, how come banks have branches?*

He decides against it.

Instead, he begs, "Oh, please. Oh, please. Oh, please. It's the best computer program ever, the graphics, the capabilities. And it only costs a couple of hundred bucks."

"A couple of hundred bucks." Mr. Martin leans back on the kitchen counter, pretending to faint and then revive. "If it's not a new game you want, it's a new computer program. If it's not that, it's a new bike. Or the latest shoes."

"I needed those shoes. They improved my basketball game," Matthew informs them.

Sighing, Mrs. Martin says, "Practice improved your game, not a pair of shoes."

"This computer program does everything." Matthew continues to plead. "Please, Mom. Please, Dad."

He gives them his best look, the one that says, *I'm your only son. I get good grades. I don't cause any major trouble, at least not the way my older sister does. I have cute brown hair that gets very red in the sun and I know that you really love my freckles.*

His best look isn't working.

Matthew's parents just shake their heads.

"Why can't you just copy the program?" Mrs. Martin asks.

"That's illegal." Matthew looks up at his father. "Dad, you're a lawyer. You know I shouldn't do that. Anyway, the company has it blocked so that no one can make a copy—and furthermore, buying the program also connects me through the modem with their special bulletin board."

Mrs. Martin sighs again.

Not a good sign, Matthew thinks. So far his parents have sighed, frowned, and shaken their heads.

Matthew's knees are beginning to hurt from kneeling. He doesn't want to give up, though.

This is all Amanda's fault, he thinks. Amanda, the sister from Hell. Life isn't fair. Amanda got born first and then she acted like a little angel for years so that he got into trouble for being the bad little brother. Then, zap, one day she stopped being a little angel and Mr. and Mrs. Martin decided to become much stricter parents. And now, Matthew is stuck trying to deal with all their new techniques.

"Don't you want me to get a good job someday? How am I going to become the best computer-game inventor if I don't have all the necessary materials? Do you want me to have no future? I'll end up jobless, with no self-esteem, with no place to go, not even a coin to phone home with to ask for help. Everyone will say, 'Those Martins. They let poor Matthew, the one with all that promise, fall by the wayside.' "

"I wish he would promise to stop nagging us." Mr. Martin grins at his wife.

She grins back and then looks down again, at Matthew. "Get up, my son. You're wearing out the knees of the new pants that you just couldn't live without."

Matthew clutches his heart and says, "My own parents."

Mrs. Martin gestures for her son to rise.

Matthew gives it one last try, staying on his knees. "Please, I beseech you, O mighty parental units, who can afford to buy a brand-new deluxe station wagon but can't afford to buy their only son a measly computer program."

Mrs. Martin starts to get annoyed. "It's not a matter of what we can afford, it's a matter of how much we want to just give you. You have no appreciation of the value of money, of how hard we have to work for it. As for that station wagon, I needed it for my business and what's more, I earned it."

She can feel her blood pressure rising.

Her son also rises.

Now it's his turn to sigh. "I'd earn my own money if I could. That's just a lot for someone my age to earn. By the time I saved up for that program, it would be out of date."

"Exactly. You're asking for something that won't be state of the art for very long. And it's not as if we haven't bought you excellent equipment."

"I know," Matthew acknowledges. "It's just that this is *such* a great program. . . ."

His parents start taking out the ingredients to make milk shakes.

Mrs. Martin takes out Tiger's Milk, wheat germ, protein powder, and oranges.

Mr. Martin takes out milk, chocolate syrup, and ice cream.

They each use their own blenders.

Matthew gazes longingly at his father's blender.

"I'll share," his father offers.

Another sigh escapes the health-conscious Mrs. Martin.

Matthew grins. "Thanks."

There's a pause as Matthew thinks, watching his father pour the mixture into glasses.

Matthew tries again. "You're sending Amanda to Camp Sarah Bernhardt. It's very expensive, right? It's an acting camp, right? I don't see why she gets to go to a camp to learn how to be an actress, which she will never earn any money doing, because she's a terrible actress. She can't even act like a human being most of the time. All I want is the money to buy a computer program, which will teach me skills that will help me earn lots of money when I grow up—that will help me to support you in your old age. I bet that someday I'll even make enough to help support Amanda in her old age after she never gets a job as an actress."

"Matthew, your sister has known for a long time that she wants to be an actress. And even if she changes her mind, this camp is a good idea for her right now." His mother pours her health drink into a glass and then stirs it with a piece of celery. "And, for your information, your sister is paying part of the camp costs. She's using money from baby-sitting, birthday presents, and saved allowance."

Thinking about how much trouble Amanda has caused, all the things that she's done in the past few months, Matthew wonders whether he should start doing some things, too, so that he can get what he wants. Maybe he should shave off all the hair on his head, pretend to get his nose pierced, spend a lot of time in his room crying the way his sister has been doing.

He decides that's not what he wants to do.

Instead he says, "I know. You love her more than you love me."

Arranging his face into a pout, lower lip slightly forward, trying hard to make the saddest face he knows how to make, Matthew waits for his parents' reaction.

Mr. and Mrs. Martin look at each other, shake their heads, and then look at their son.

Matthew tries to hold the look but starts to smile.

Handing his son a milk shake, Mr. Martin says, "Enough already. You're not going to wear us down this time. Matthew, we're not going to spend hundreds of dollars on something that we're not even sure that you're going to use. We know that you like computers, but you haven't been using ours the way that you used to."

Now Matthew feels really frustrated. "When I played computer games all the time, you told me to get out and be with my friends. Now I do that. But I still want to work with the computer, and this program is really the most advanced one ever."

"Matthew, over the years we've spent a lot of money on things that you just couldn't live without and then once we bought them, you lost interest." His father sounds very irritated.

His mother continues. "What about the remote-control car you *had* to have but never play with anymore? What about all of those computer games that you think are too easy now? What about the clothes you just had to have and won't wear anymore?"

Matthew tries to defend himself. "Mom, I'm too old for some of those things now. The games *are* too easy. *No one* plays with remote-control cars anymore. And what am I supposed to do, keep wearing my old Smurf clothes forever?"

"Matthew"—his mother starts to smile—"you know that I'm not talking about Smurf clothes."

Matthew's getting more and more frustrated.

Why can't his parents see that he's not a little kid anymore?

He takes a few minutes to think, slurping on his straw as he finishes his milk shake.

"I've got an idea," Matthew says. "What if I can earn half of the money—will you contribute the other half?"

His parents look at each other, doing their Martin parents telepathic thing, and both nod yes at the same time.

"All right!" Matthew sticks his fist into the air.

Now all he's got to do is figure out how to earn the money—and show his parents that he really is growing up.

Chapter 2

```
*  *  *  *  *  *  *  *  *  *  *  *  *  *  *  *  *  *  *  *  *
*                    ROOM TO RENT                          *
*                                                          *
*                 NEED A PLACE TO STAY                     *
*               IN SCENIC CALIFON, N.J.?                   *
*   Room available for summer months in a really          *
*   nice house, while sister is away at drama              *
*   camp. During year it is used by a demented             *
*   but neat thirteen-year-old. COST: Half the             *
*   price of computer program that renter can't            *
```

```
*    live without.                             *
*    EXTRA ADDED ATTRACTIONS—Very healthy      *
*    food served (especially if you like sprouty tofu  *
*    —if not, my father and I will share our very  *
*    excellent hidden supply of junk food). For a  *
*    little bit more money you can wear previous  *
*    occupant's weird clothes. (All different be-  *
*    cause she is "trying to find out who the real  *
*    Amanda Martin is." I can tell you: She's a  *
*    Barfburger.)                               *
*            CONTACT MATTHEW MARTIN             *
*                 AT (908)555-1144              *
*  *  *  *  *  *  *  *  *  *  *  *  *  *  *  *  *  *  *  *
```

"What a doofus." Joshua Jackson stares at his best friend. "You can't rent out your sister's room."

"Give me one good reason." Matthew sits down on a picnic table at the recreation field. "Just give me one good reason."

Joshua starts counting on his fingers. "One, Amanda is still at home. She doesn't leave for camp for three more days. Two, your parents will never allow a stranger to stay in the house. Three, the neighborhood isn't zoned for hotels. Four, your parents will not think that renting out a room in the house that *they* pay a mortgage on is what they meant when they said that you had to *work* for your half of the payment."

"I said, just give me *one* good reason." Matthew folds the ad for renting the room into a paper airplane.

"Five," Joshua continues, "you are really a doofoid if you think that Amanda won't kill you for renting out her room."

"I'm willing to share the profits with her." Matthew throws the paper plane at Joshua. "Ninety percent for me, ten percent for her. Lately, she's been threatening to move out on her own. This way she'll earn something without having to do anything. And this will give her some money to use at camp. And she won't even be around to have to deal with the stranger I rent her room to. *I'm* the one who will have to deal with the stranger."

"Stranger is what you get every day," Joshua kids. "You know that your family wouldn't go along with this scheme. Why don't you just buy a cheaper program? There are a lot of them you can get."

Matthew shakes his head. "Not one like this. With this program I can make holograms, produce animated features, link up with a modem to a program with the best computer programmers on line—"

"Okay, okay." Joshua stops him. "Enough already. I believe you. For someone who is always fooling around, you really do take this stuff seriously."

Wishing that his parents realized how serious he is about the program, Matthew nods and then gets hit on the head by a basketball.

Tyler White rushes over. "I'm sorry. Are you all right?"

Feeling his head for bumps and blood, Matthew says, "I think so."

Billy Kellerman also rushes over. "Let me help. Do you have a concussion? A subdermal hematoma?"

"I'm fine." Matthew does not want Billy to do anything.

Billy comes closer, touching Matthew on the head. "I'm going to be a doctor, remember? I'm a doctor's son. Let me help you."

"Checking for head lice?" Vanessa Singer stops by the table and makes a face at Matthew.

Matthew looks at her and snarls. "If he was looking for lice—or more likely, a louse—he would have come straight to you."

"Maybe Billy's going to become a psychiatrist. That's why he's examining your head." Vanessa laughs at her own joke.

Matthew stares at the person with whom he has a mutual torment society and says, "If he's a head-shrinker, he certainly would have no reason to check you out—pea brain."

"He's got you." Joshua licks his finger and acts like he's keeping score on an air scoreboard.

Rubbing his sore head, Matthew looks at Vanessa and says, "Why don't you just mind your own business? Why did you come over here? I wasn't bothering you."

"Not this time." Vanessa gets ready to list all of the times that Matthew has bothered her.

Matthew cuts her off by saying, "Look. If you've come over here because you want to play doctor with Billy, why don't you just say so?"

11

Billy pretends to take a stethoscope out of an imaginary medical bag.

Blushing, Vanessa says, "You boys are such pigs."

As she leaves, the boys start to oink and snort.

"You're so mean to her." Jil! Hudson walks up to them. "She'll never forget this moment of torment as long as she lives. When she comes back to the fiftieth reunion of our graduation from sixth grade, she'll still remember how you all oinked and snorted at her."

The boys all stare at Jil!, whose high sense of drama caused her to change the second *l* in her name to an exclamation point and who, her parents tell her, "makes mountains out of molehills."

"They don't have reunions for sixth-grade graduations," Matthew reminds her. "And she started it."

"She did." Joshua sticks up for his friend.

Tyler grabs his basketball, makes sure that there's no blood on it and that Matthew has not dented it, and heads back to the basketball court.

Billy and Joshua follow him, leaving Jil! and Matthew alone at the table.

Jil! sits down and looks at the field by the school. "Just think. By this time next week the summer recreation program will be here and I'll be stuck up at the lake, watching my bratty little brother and waiting for my mother to give birth to another future person who I will have to baby-sit."

"Are they going to pay you?" Matthew asks.

Jil! nods. "Yeah. But not enough for all that I have to do, especially now."

"Can I borrow the money that you make? There's this really great computer program that I have to have and my parents won't—"

Jil! lightly slugs him on the arm. "Matthew Martin. You already owe me money for the last movie that we went to. I don't mind paying for myself, although I have heard rumors that in some cultures boys actually sometimes pay for their date's tickets. And anyway, I want to use that money to buy myself some clothes for seventh grade so that my mother can't always tell me what to wear."

"But it's a great program. I'll even let you use it." Matthew puts his hand on the hand that has just lightly slugged him on the arm.

Jil!, knowing how much computers mean to Matthew, realizes that he has just paid her a great compliment. She also likes having his hand on hers, but she is not going to give in. "No, Matthew. I'm not going to loan you the money. You know that you owe half the kids in sixth grade money and that you never pay it back."

Matthew nods, knowing that she's not going to give in, knowing also that it's not half the class that he owes money to, but three quarters of it.

Jil! changes the subject. "Are you going to miss me when I go away? After all, I'm going to be gone most of the summer."

Matthew continues to think about how he's going to get the money that he needs for the program.

13

Jil! takes his hand off her hand and sticks out her lower lip. "Answer. Aren't you going to miss me?"

Matthew looks at Jil!, remembering how just a few months ago, he thought that all girls were slug slime and how different it's been now that he likes her. He also thinks about how he's been discovering how much more fun it is to kiss a girl than kiss a relative and how until just recently he and Jil! have talked about spending the summer learning to become really good kissers by practicing a lot.

But her parents have decided that renting a cabin at the lake will be restful for Mrs. Hudson, who is very pregnant and "wants to just stick her feet in the water."

It doesn't seem fair to Matthew that Mr. and Mrs. Hudson have ruined Jil!'s and Matthew's kissing plan and they don't even know about it.

It also doesn't seem fair to Matthew that Mr. and Mrs. Hudson have ruined Jil! and Matthew's kissing plan when they have obviously been doing some kissing of their own.

Matthew, even though he is not absolutely positive of all of the steps that caused the future Baby Hudson, knows that his and Jil!'s plans don't go that far. In fact, they secretly call the plan "Elementary Lips."

Matthew wishes that Mrs. Hudson would just stick her feet in the home bathtub instead of having to go to the lake.

"Are you going to miss me?" Jil! repeats.

Matthew, realizing that he really *is* going to miss

her, nods and thinks about how quickly some things change when you're growing up.

And then he thinks about how slowly other things change, about how hard it is to convince his parents that he really is growing up, and how it's sometimes hard for him to think about growing up, and how Elementary Lips was doomed before it even started.

He stops thinking when Jil! leans over and gives him a quick kiss, when no one on the playground is watching.

Suddenly summer seems a long, long time.

Chapter 3

"Why do I have to set the table?" Amanda slams the dishes down. "How come that little turd-le brain never has to do anything?"

"I set the table last night. And anyway, they like me better than they like you," Matthew informs her, and then turns to his parents, who are preparing two kinds of salad dressing, cucumber yogurt and Russian. "Did you hear what she called me—turd?"

"I said turT-le." Amanda looks smug.

"Whose idea was it to have children anyway?"

Mr. Martin mixes the mayonnaise with ketchup. "Honey, would you please refresh my memory?"

Mrs. Martin adds caraway seeds to her dressing. "I think it was my mother's idea. She kept clutching her heart and saying, 'When will I have grandchildren? What if I die before I hear some sweet little voice saying, "Grammy, I love you"?' So we decided to do it for her and then she moved to Florida. Now our children call her and say, 'Thanks for the check,' and 'Grammy, I love you,' and then we have them the rest of the time."

"We should have gotten a parrot instead. Over the phone she would never have known the difference." Mr. Martin adds more mayonnaise to his dressing.

"You two think you are so funny." Amanda slams another dish down on the table. "You're always telling us how much you wanted to have us and now you're making up this dumb story just to be funny. Why does everything always have to be a joke with you? I can't wait to get to drama camp, where all I have to do is study acting and not be treated like a waitress and not always have you kidding around."

Mr. Martin taste-tests his dressing and adds a little more mayonnaise to it. "Someday you're going to thank us for making you set the table. Most people who want to be actresses end up waiting on tables at some point in their careers."

Amanda sticks her nose up in the air.

Matthew thinks about lobbing a spoonful of mayonnaise into it.

"Let's all sit down and have a peaceful dinner," Mrs. Martin pleads. "Tonight is Amanda's last night with us and I want it to go well."

Amanda looks at her watch and says, "I'm going out to meet some friends after dinner."

"Be home by ten," Mrs. Martin tells her. "You've got to finish packing and you're going to have to get up very early tomorrow."

Amanda sighs but nods yes.

"So what's new?" Mr. Martin asks, once everyone is seated and has started to eat.

"New York . . . New Jersey . . . New Hampshire . . . New Monia," Matthew answers.

"Can't you tell him not to be such a dork?" Amanda looks at her parents.

"I said New York, not New Dork." Matthew takes a forkful of mashed potatoes.

Mr. Martin decides to change the subject. "Do you know yet what plays they will be doing at camp?"

Shaking her head, Amanda watches as Matthew puts the mashed potatoes into his mouth and tries to blow a bubble with them.

Choosing to ignore him, she continues. "They don't announce it ahead of time anymore because some of the kids used to come to camp with the parts that they wanted totally memorized. Some of them even worked with their own drama coaches before they got there, and that wasn't fair to the other kids."

"Are you nervous?" Mrs. Martin says softly.

Suddenly Amanda doesn't seem so angry. She nods, quietly.

"It'll work out okay." Mrs. Martin pats her daughter's hand and remembers how hard it was growing up.

"I really want to go, get away from here," Amanda says.

"Are we that terrible as parents?" Mr. Martin says, thinking about all of the family counseling sessions they have attended.

"No," Amanda says softly. "It's just everything. *Nothing's* gone right this year. I don't know who I am. I don't know why Danny broke up with me. I don't know why everything seems so hard all of a sudden. No. You're not *that* terrible as parents."

Matthew asks, "Am I that terrible as a younger brother?"

She nods and grins.

Matthew grins back. "Good. I do my best."

"If you want to come home from camp, don't be afraid to tell us. You can come home anytime," Mr. Martin says.

There goes the chance to rent out her room, Matthew thinks.

"But don't give up too easily, either, honey. I bet that this is going to be a great summer for you," Mrs. Martin reassures her.

"I hope so." Amanda finishes eating and looks at her watch. "Is it okay if I go now so that I can see my friends and be back by ten?"

Mrs. Martin is unsure. "The person who sets is supposed to clean up also."

Matthew volunteers. "I'll do it."

Everyone looks at him unbelievingly.

"I've been possessed by a demon," he kids. "Tomorrow we can call an exorcist. Tonight I'll clean up."

"Are you going to try to make me pay for this?" Amanda wants to know.

Matthew shakes his head.

Mrs. Martin looks on in disbelief.

Mr. Martin, who loves an old television show called *Leave It to Beaver*, picks up his plate and says, "Well, Beav, you certainly are being nice to your sibling. Let me help you clear this table."

As the Martin men clean up, they hum the theme music to *Leave It to Beaver*.

Amanda leaves, mumbling, "This is some kind of plot to make me miss them, to make me be homesick, to not let me try to separate and become my own person. It's not going to work."

Drying the dishes, Matthew thinks about how, in less than twenty-four hours, he's practically going to be an only child, about how his first and only sort of girlfriend is going away for the summer, and about how he's already gotten enough advances on his allowance to keep him broke until school starts in September.

And the summer is just beginning.

Chapter 4

"Well, here we are. Another summer at the recreation program. New grounds, new equipment, same old stuff for the little kids to make." Matthew sits down on a table and picks up some of the pot holders left behind by some of the six- to eight-year-old campers. "Do you think I could pay those kids a quarter for each of these and then sell them for fifty cents?"

"Not another money-making scheme." Billy pretends to yawn. "That's all we've heard about lately."

Holding up a fluorescent pot holder, Matthew

says, "I bet someone would pay fifty cents for this. My mother always paid that for mine."

Lisa takes the pot holder from his hand. "She bought it because she's your mother and it's a parent thing to do, to buy misshapen, loosely looped, and mis-woven pot holders from their kids. But no one, except for a relative or a neighbor of the kid who made the stupid pot holder, will *buy* the stupid pot holder."

Matthew tries to think of other ways to earn money.

Lisa looks around the table at everyone who has gathered. "So where are all of the soon-to-be seventh graders?" she asks. "Inquiring minds want to know."

Zoe Alexander tosses her blond hair. "I know. I know."

"Zoe spends half her life on the telephone." Tyler White puts his arm around Zoe's waist.

"But the other half I devote to you." Zoe puts her head on his shoulder. "I have since we first started to go together."

Oh, puke, Matthew thinks.

Zoe begins her list of classmate whereabouts. "Jil!, as Matthew knows so well, has just left for the lake."

"She'd rather jump in the lake than be around him for the summer." Vanessa looks up from the lanyard she is making.

"I hope that's a noose you're working on, one for *your* neck." Matthew glares at her.

"Lighten up, you guys. All of this fighting is get-ting very boring." Billy pretends to yawn.

"She started it," Matthew says, thinking about how many times he has used that phrase, first about his sister Amanda and now about Vanessa.

Zoe ignores them, continuing her report. "Lizzie's spending the summer with her father and his family in Montana. Jessica and her family are going driving cross-country, camping out."

Matthew thinks about how much he likes teasing Jessica and her family about their last name, which is Weeks, and says, "As soon as they left town, the summer in Califon got shorter, since four Weeks are now gone."

People groan and Vanessa says, "That is just so lame."

"Sarah and her horse have gone off to riding camp. Katie and her bike are part of a tour around the Grand Canyon. I spoke to her last week and the blisters on her feet have blisters." Zoe giggles.

"Your phone bill must be so gigantic." Ryma Browne shakes her head.

"It's part of the divorce settlement. My mother's lawyer negotiated it so that I could make all the phone calls I wanted and my father would pay them," Zoe explains. "To continue, although I have not heard directly from the boys, since most of them hate to use the phone, I can only give you some information: David Cohen has gone to space camp and then his parents are driving cross-country. He'll be back soon. Patrick's parents' divorce went through and his mom is making him move away to where she's going. Pablo is going to

Puerto Rico to spend the summer with his grandparents."

"And I'm watching his snakes." Mark Ellison walks up to the table. "And here they are, Boa'd with school and Vindshield Viper."

Most of the girls scream and run off, except for Vanessa, who mumbles, "How immature," Cathy Atwood, who likes snakes, and Zoe, who goes "Eek! Eek!" and falls into Tyler's arms.

"I'm taking them for a walk," Mark informs all of those who are left.

"Don't you mean 'taking them for a slither'?" Matthew grins. "Where are their collars? Do they have a new leash on life?"

"That was a very dumb joke, very dumb." Vanessa makes a thumbs-down gesture.

"For once I agree." Joshua holds his nose. "That joke stinks."

Zoe moves out of Tyler's embrace and puts his arm around her waist. "And our next-door neighbor, Daniella, told me that her niece, Lacey, and her nephew, Jimmy, will be visiting for the summer while their parents are building houses for some group."

"How old are her niece and nephew? Are they old enough to be on our baseball team?" Tyler is always trying to get the best team together.

"The girl is our age. And the boy, I think, is a little younger."

Tyler takes his arm away from Zoe's waist and

swings an imaginary baseball bat. "I hope that they're good. I want our rec team to be the best."

"I'll be the best cheerleader." Zoe tilts her head and places Tyler's arm back around her waist.

"I know just what the cheer should be." Matthew gets up from the table and pretends that he is holding on to pom-poms. "Give Me a *B* . . . an *A* . . . an *R* . . . an *F* . . . What do they spell . . . ?"

"I shudder to think about what he's going to be like with Jil! away. She was such a good influence." Zoe looks at Matthew, who has just fallen in the dirt trying to do a cartwheel.

Matthew gets up, wipes off the dust, and thinks about how boring it gets during the summer when there's no place to go and not much to do.

Someone, he thinks, *has got to make things exciting.*

And then he thinks, *That someone is me. This is going to be a Matthew Martin summer production. . . . Tune in tomorrow.*

Chapter 5

"All right, you guys. You think that this is your turf? Well, I'm here to tell you it's not. Your days are numbered." Matthew tries to sound like the hero of every action movie he has ever seen. "I'm the one who's gonna cut you down to size."

There's not a sound from his opposition.

Matthew continues. "You think you can just sprout up where you want and exhibit your blades and that everyone will just let you grow freely, run wild over this land? Well, I'm the man who's gonna mow you down."

There's still not a sound from his opposition.

"Scared, huh?" Matthew speaks menacingly. "Well, you should be. I'm gonna run circles around you and cut you down in your prime."

Matthew finishes mowing his initials into the grass and then continues work on Mrs. Levy's lawn.

"This is so boring. It takes a lot to make it interesting." He thinks about how many neighborhood lawns he's mowed lately and about how it's taking so long to earn the money he needs. Then he accidentally runs the mower into a cow lawn-ornament, one of those fuzzy cloth things that look like there's a midget bovine munching on the grass.

"Sorry. You should have moooooooooooooooooved over." Matthew starts to laugh.

He looks up at the house to make sure that Mrs. Levy, the "Cow Collector of Califon," hasn't seen him almost run over the large ornament.

It's a shame we don't live in Cowlifon, Matthew thinks.

"Matthew," Mrs. Levy calls from the house.

Oh, no, he thinks, *she's seen me. It's an udder disaster.*

"Matthew." Mrs. Levy repeats her call.

Turning off the lawn mower, Matthew heads up the hill to her house.

As he walks past the cow mailbox, he thinks about how he's almost done with the mowing and now he's

27

going to have to use the money that he's earned to pay for repairing the cow.

Mrs. Levy is looking a little frantic.

Matthew thinks of what his father always says— "Don't have a cow over this"—and hopes that Mrs. Levy doesn't have one because he ran the "lawn mooer" over her yard ornament.

Mrs. Levy is very nervous. "Matthew, I've just gotten a call from my friend who lives a few blocks away. She's had an accident carving up a turkey and wants me to come over immediately. Theo and the baby are taking a nap, and I think it would be easier and faster if I left them here for the few minutes I will be gone. Would you mind baby-sitting for them until I get back? I'll only be gone a few minutes."

A few minutes—easy, a piece of cake, Matthew thinks, and says, "Sure."

Mrs. Levy doesn't look very confident. "Matthew, are you certain you can handle this?"

Matthew gives her what he hopes is his most competent look. "Yes, I can."

"The baby is very young, only two months old. Maybe I should take her with me, but I hope I'll be back before she even wakes up. It's just around the corner. I've written down the number and put it next to the phone with all of the other emergency numbers."

The phone rings.

Mrs. Levy picks it up. "I'm on my way. Don't panic. I'll be right there."

Putting down the phone, Mrs. Levy looks at Matthew and says, "Are you sure you can handle this?"

Matthew nods. "I can always call my mother if there's a problem."

"Promise." Mrs. Levy keeps walking to the door and back again.

"I promise." Matthew opens the kitchen door. "It'll be all right. I'm very mature for my age."

At least I'm very mature for my age right this second, Matthew almost adds, but realizes that a joke at this time is a very bad idea.

Mrs. Levy says, "Look, Matthew. My friend is a bit of a hypochondriac. She's a big worrier. So all this is going to take, I hope, is my going over there, looking at the cut, telling her that she's going to live, and then coming right back here. This is not the first time something like this has happened."

"I'll be glad to help out," Matthew says, thinking, *What can go wrong?*

Mrs. Levy stands there for a minute and then makes a decision and leaves, telling Matthew that she'll be back in just a few minutes.

Matthew is left alone in the house with two children, who he hopes stay asleep until their mother returns.

He decides to check out what kind of junk food is in the refrigerator.

Just as he gets to the refrigerator door, he stops and thinks about how he wants his parents to see him as grown up and responsible.

Going straight to the refrigerator does not seem the best way to prove it, so he goes to the phone to call his mother.

Matthew wants to let his mother know that Mrs. Levy thinks that he is grown up enough to handle an emergency.

He also wants to make sure that his mother is on alert in case he needs to call her for help.

Matthew picks up the phone, which is shaped like a cow lying in a pasture.

Picking up the top part, he holds it up to his ear.

It feels weird, as if any minute the cow is going to start leaking milk into his ear.

Oh, well, he thinks, *I guess it's time to cowll my mother and tell her what's happening.*

He dials, the phone rings, and his mother answers. "Martin's Missives. May I help you?"

"Mom, it's me." Matthew can feel the cow-tail yarn tickle his chin. "Don't worry. It's no gigantic emergency. I just have to tell you something."

"Are you sure that everything's okay? I have a customer on the other line, but I'll ask her to wait if it's an emergency."

"I can wait," Matthew informs her.

Mrs. Martin switches back to her other phone call, putting Matthew on hold.

Being on hold means having to listen to a taped message about his mother's company.

Matthew listens to how a person can hire a person dressed in a costume to deliver a gift or message.

He wonders if anyone has ever sent Mrs. Levy a messenger dressed as a cow. He debates sending her someone in a boy cow costume, along with a message saying, "Your collection is really a lot of bull," but decides that wouldn't be very good for his own business and he really does want the new computer software.

Mrs. Martin gets back on the phone. "Okay, honey. What's happening?"

Matthew explains about Mrs. Levy's emergency and how he's watching her two still-sleeping children.

"Honey, you've never been around a baby for any amount of time. Do you know what to do?"

"It's not hard. I watched Jill practice on an old doll, so I can feed the kid and burp it." Matthew takes the cow tail on the end of the phone and puts it on his upper lip, pretending it's a mustache.

That makes him feel older and much more competent.

Mrs. Martin sighs. "I wish that I could come over and help, but I've got to watch the store and answer the phone. If this is an emergency, I will close down and come over."

"Mom. This is *not* an emergency. What do you think I am? A baby?" Matthew feels that, once again, he isn't given enough credit.

"Okay." Mrs. Martin decides to let Matthew handle the situation, although she's nervous.

She spends the next five minutes telling him how to hold the baby, what to do if the baby starts to cry, how to change the diaper, and how to warm up for-mula.

Suddenly a telephone operator comes in on the call and explains that Mrs. Levy wants to talk to him.

Matthew says good-bye to his mother and hello to Mrs. Levy, who is frantic because the telephone line has been busy for so long.

"Matthew, is everything all right? Please. I don't want you to stay on the phone talking to your friends." She sounds upset. "Are the children all right?"

Matthew starts to get annoyed and then remem-bers that he mowed into her cow, and if she knows about that, she probably thinks that he's going to do that to her kids.

He explains that he was talking to his mother, get-ting instructions on the care, feeding, and diapering of babies.

"And, Mrs. Levy," he informs her, "Mom says if there is a big problem, she'll close the store and come over here immediately."

There's a huge sigh of relief from the other side of the phone.

Mrs. Levy explains that her friend has cut herself very badly and they are rushing to the hospital. Then she gives him the number in the emergency room and makes him promise to take good care of her children.

Matthew promises.

After the phone call is over, Matthew goes into the baby's room and looks at the sleeping two-month-old.

Putting his finger in front of her nose, Matthew checks to make sure that she is breathing.

She is.

He walks into Theo's room.

Theo is awake and jumping up and down on his bed.

Matthew thinks about how much fun it would be to join him, but then remembers that he is now in charge and that would probably not be such a good idea.

Theo stops jumping and asks for his mother.

Matthew explains that she's gone out for a few minutes and Theo starts to cry.

Matthew tells him not to worry.

Theo continues to cry.

"Want to read a book? Watch television? Play baseball?"

More crying from Theo. "I want my mommy."

There's a moment when Matthew thinks about how he wants his mommy, too, to help him out of this dilemma, but then he starts offering more choices.

"How about playing a game? Doing a puzzle? Looking under the sofa cushions for loose change?"

Theo is still crying.

"How about looking in the refrigerator for something good to eat?" Matthew suggests.

Theo stops yelling, "Mommy. Mommy. Mommy," and says, "Ice cream."

"If it's in the freezer, it's ours." Matthew smiles.

The boys head into the kitchen, look in the refrigerator, and discover a carton of Cherry Garcia.

In three minutes they are eating the ice cream and
quietly watching television.

Matthew is sitting there, proud that he has han-
dled the situation so well, even though he knows that
neither of the moms will be overjoyed by the consumption of junk food.

He thinks about how easy this is going to be.

The phone rings.

It's Mrs. Levy, again checking to make sure that
her children are all right.

The phone wakes up the baby.

And the crying really starts.

Chapter 6

Matthew and Theo stare down at the screaming baby.

"I guess she won't shut up if I give her Cherry Garcia," Matthew says.

"My mother usually breast-feeds her when she wakes up," Theo tells him.

"No way." Matthew shakes his head.

Theo giggles.

"How old are you?" Matthew asks him.

Theo holds up one hand. "This many." He has four fingers raised.

"Well, you remember this better than I do. It was done to you more recently. What did your mother do to stop you from crying?"

"I already told you." Theo sticks his thumb into his mouth.

"The formula," Matthew remembers.

He heads to the refrigerator and takes out a bottle, trying to remember about warming it up.

Matthew holds the bottle in his hands, staring at it with all sorts of questions in his head. *How hot do I make it? How do I warm it up? Can it be nuked? What happened to the nipple on the bottle?*

In the background he can hear the baby screaming.

Theo stands in front of him. "More ice cream."

"Not now," Matthew tells him.

Theo starts to cry.

"Not now," Matthew pleads.

"Now." Theo stamps his foot.

"No ice cream now. No crying now," Matthew demands.

Theo drops to the floor and starts pounding on it.

In the background the baby seems to be screaming even louder.

Matthew rushes into the living room, where he remembers having seen a portable non–cow phone and quickly calls his mother.

"Martin's Missives."

"Mom. I need help. Everyone's crying except me

. . . so far," he tells her. "Theo is throwing a temper tantrum because I said he couldn't have any more ice cream."

"*You* said no more ice cream?" she exclaims. "Let me mark this date on my calendar."

"Mom, this is no time for sarcasm. I'm having a major problem here." Matthew moves toward the baby's room, holding on to the cold bottle of formula.

Reaching the crib, he says to his mother, "Here. I want you to listen to this." He holds the phone next to the screaming baby.

Then he gets back on the phone. "Mom, why is she crying like that? She's been doing that since she woke up."

"Remember what I told you earlier? Did you pick her up? Give her warm milk? Check to see if her diaper needs changing?" Mrs. Martin asks.

"No, I didn't do any of those things," he says.

"Put down the phone for a minute and pick her up carefully. I'll wait to see what happens."

Matthew puts down the phone and carefully lifts up the baby, who continues to cry.

He lays her down and picks up the phone again. "I guess she doesn't find me charming."

"Look in her diaper. See if she's wet or something."

"Do I have to?" Matthew starts to whine.

"Yes."

Matthew checks. "She's wet—*and* something."

His mother chuckles.

"This is not funny. This is gross. Couldn't they have house-trained her?"

This is so disgusting, Matthew thinks as he looks at the contents of the diaper he's just changed. *What have they been feeding this kid? Cream of baked beans?*

Matthew finishes the job, leaving the dirty Pamper in the crib.

He wipes the baby ointment off his hands onto his jeans and gets back on the phone. "Mission accomplished."

"Put the diaper in the garbage," his mother tells him.

Matthew can't figure out how she knows things she cannot see.

Mrs. Martin then reminds Matthew how to warm up the bottle, how to feed and burp the baby.

"Call me once everything is done and let me know how it's going," she says.

"If nothing works, would you please come over here?" he begs.

"Yes. But I have faith in you that you can handle this," she informs him, and then hangs up. She worries again but decides to wait and see.

Over at the Levy house Matthew feels like his only line to the outside world is gone and he's caught in Baby-sitter Hell.

The baby continues to cry and Theo is running around the room pretending to be an airplane.

Matthew picks the baby up and sings every song he knows to her. Finally, the fifth time he has hummed the theme song from *Leave It to Beaver* to her, she quiets down and starts looking at her fingernails.

Theo leaves the room, yelling, "I'm going to land now and refuel."

Matthew looks at the baby's fingernails and wonders how anything can be that small and wonders when those hands will be old enough to change someone else's diapers or her own.

He puts her back into the crib and goes back into the kitchen.

Theo is sitting at the kitchen table, eating ice cream straight out of the container.

Matthew wonders if he should get a spoon and join him.

Theo looks up at him and then spits into the carton. "All mine."

Matthew at first is disgusted, and then marvels at Theo's way of getting all the ice cream. He wonders why he never thought of doing that so that Amanda would not want the ice cream.

Still angry at Matthew for having said no, Theo is making up a song about how he's going to chop Matthew up and feed him to the cows.

Ignoring Theo, Matthew tries to remember everything his mother told him. First warm up water in a pan. Then fix the bottle so that the nipple is outside. Then put the bottle into the pan, making sure that it is no longer heating up. When it seems ready, sprinkle a little of the formula on the wrist to make sure that it isn't too hot or too cold, that it's just right.

While he's waiting, Matthew looks around the kitchen. There are cow salt and pepper shakers, cow napkin rings, a cow creamer.

Matthew thinks about that. If the manufacturers were being accurate, the milk should not be coming out of the cow's mouth.

Matthew continues to look around. Cow mugs. Cow prints on the wall. A cow butter dish. A cow calendar. Cow egg cups.

Since when do cows come from eggs? Matthew wonders.

The milk is ready.

Matthew is not sure that he is ready to feed the baby, but he goes back into her bedroom.

She's still there.

Theo walks in and watches as Matthew puts down the bottle, picks up the baby, sits down in the chair, and realizes that he can't reach the bottle.

"Theo, please hand me the bottle," Matthew asks.

Theo looks at him. "I'll give it to you if you promise to buy me snot bubble gum."

"What?" Matthew yells.

The baby starts to cry.

Matthew looks down, rocks her a little, and then looks back at Theo. "Snot bubble gum?"

"Yeah. My mommy said it was a waste of money and disgusting and I want it. It's a nose and you pull back this thing and snot bubble gum comes through the holes in the nose," Theo explains.

Matthew wonders why he's missed out on this

nifty item. "Okay. Hand me the bottle and I'll get one for each of us."

Theo hands him the bottle, which Matthew then puts in the baby's mouth.

"It's not doing anything. Nothing's coming out." Matthew is feeling frustrated.

The baby starts to cry.

He takes the bottle out of the baby's mouth and holding it up to his face to look at it, he squeezes the nipple.

Milk squirts into his eye.

"Here goes." Blinking, Matthew puts the bottle back in the baby's mouth. "Yo, ho, ho and a bottle of formula. Drink up or ye'll have to walk the plank."

Pirate movies are another of his favorites.

The milk goes into the baby.

Matthew can also feel the milk come out of the baby.

It's streaming out of the diaper leg that he didn't make tight enough.

Matthew's lap is wet.

He sits there thinking about how he hopes that no one sees him going home.

Matthew remembers that he's got to burp the baby.

Carefully picking the baby up, he puts her on his shoulder, forgetting to place a cloth on his shoulder.

Patting her softly on her back, he starts to sing to her. "The worms crawl in, the worms crawl out, the worms play pinochle on your snout."

Theo listens, learning the words, and then joins in.

Matthew keeps patting the baby on the back.

The baby makes a little popping sound from her mouth.

"Mission accomplished." Matthew feels proud of himself until he feels a little stream of warm liquid running down his neck and into his T-shirt.

Picking the baby up, he puts her back into the crib and goes into the bathroom to take a look.

As he walks, he can feel the liquid trickling down his shoulder and onto his chest.

He can also hear the baby start to cry.

Matthew walks into the bathroom, takes off his shirt, and tries to clean it off by wetting a piece of toilet paper and rubbing it across the shirt. Soon there are wet, linty pieces of paper attached to it.

Taking more toilet paper, he wets it and wipes the liquid off his body.

Just as he is putting on his wet, linty shirt, Theo walks in.

"Come play trucks with me." Theo tugs at Matthew's shirt and then wrinkles his nose. "Oh, you smell."

"Thank you for sharing that with me." Matthew glares down at him.

Theo says, "My daddy puts something on to make him smell good."

He points to a bottle on the shelf.

Matthew realizes that it is the same stuff that his

father uses and debates whether there is a rule about baby-sitters being able to use cologne.

He decides that if there is a rule, it should be yes, the baby-sitter may use the cologne if the baby-sitter smells like baby poop and puke, and didn't come into the house smelling like that.

Matthew uses the cologne, putting some on his shoulder, his chest, his neck, anyplace that he thinks may have been touched by baby puke, and then, as a final touch, puts some under his armpits.

"Me too." Theo grabs Matthew's knee.

The baby is still crying in the background, so Matthew quickly puts some on Theo.

They go back into the baby's room.

This time Matthew puts a cloth on his shoulder, picks up the baby, and sits down.

The baby sticks her fingers in his eye.

Matthew manages not to say the bad word that is in his brain.

He's got to bribe Theo with another snot bubble gum to get him to bring over the bottle.

Soon, everything is quiet.

The baby is again drinking the bottle.

Theo's on the floor, playing with his entire collection of trucks. "Vroom. Vroom. Vroom. Vroom."

Also on the floor is a tiny metal herd of cattle.

"Vroom. Vroom. Vroom. You cows stop having babies." Theo drives a dump truck into the herd.

Matthew talks to the baby. Not sure of what her

interests are, he teaches her soccer rules and regulations, using a silly voice.

The baby laughs and laughs.

"What's your sister's name?" he asks Theo.

"Spot the Dog" is the answer.

"Theo, be serious." Matthew grins, remembering how he likes to call his own sister Godzilla.

"Her name is Cleo." Mrs. Levy walks into the room and looks very relieved that her children are alive and well.

She picks Cleo up.

"Watch out. She's leaking," Matthew tells her.

"She does that." Mrs. Levy smiles at him.

"Actually, she seems to leak from a lot of places." Matthew is relieved that Mrs. Levy is back and that her children are alive and well.

"I know." Mrs. Levy nods. "How did it go?"

"Okay, I guess," Matthew tells her. "It got easier after a while."

"Anything I should know?"

Matthew decides to tell her. "I put the diaper in the little garbage pail. All of your ice cream is gone. And if it isn't, I don't think it's a good idea for the rest of the family to eat it."

"It was an accidental spit." Theo looks at the floor.

Mrs. Levy looks at Matthew. "That's a new trick he's learned in nursery school. Something tells me that Theo is not totally happy not being an only child."

"I can understand that," Matthew says.

"Do you spit in the food too?" Theo asks.

"Big boys don't spit in their food," Matthew informs him.

Theo stares up at Matthew as if he's a hero. "Well, I won't either anymore."

"Thank you. Thank you. Thank you," Mrs. Levy whispers to Matthew.

Suddenly Matthew feels very grown up.

"How's your friend?" he asks.

Mrs. Levy says, "She's going to be all right. It was very messy and scary for a few minutes. The cut was very deep and took several stitches to close. No more electric carving knives for her."

Theo points to his mother's clothes and says, "Boo-boo."

Matthew notices that there is some blood on Mrs. Levy's clothes.

Patting Theo on the head, Mrs. Levy says, "Don't worry. It's not Mommy's boo-boo. I'm not hurt."

Mrs. Levy speaks to Matthew again. "I'm very glad that I didn't take the children with me. It was not an easy situation."

Matthew tries to imagine what it was like.

Theo tugs on Matthew's leg. "Don't tell her about what you promised me."

Mrs. Levy says, "What?"

"Not snot bubble gum," Theo tells her.

"Is it? Did you?" Mrs. Levy asks.

Matthew does not like having to tell on Theo.

Mrs. Levy lets him off the hook. "You've done a

good job. It's all right. Don't worry. I'll get him one the next time we go to the store."

"Two. He promised me two noses." Theo holds up two fingers.

Mrs. Levy sighs but nods.

Matthew decides to confess about a few things. "I accidentally ran into the cow on your front lawn with the mower. It's okay, just a little bald in one spot. I'll pay for the damage."

"Don't worry. My husband actually *ran* over it once with the mower, so it already was damaged. He appears to be getting a little tired of my cow obsession."

"I can't understand why." Matthew tries to look serious and then he starts to laugh.

Mrs. Levy laughs too. "Anything else I should know?"

"That's about it." Matthew tries to remember if there's anything else. "Oh, and I had to use some of your husband's cologne."

"I noticed." Mrs. Levy smiles. "Let me guess. Cleo threw up on you."

Matthew nods. "And leaked."

Mrs. Levy smiles and then takes out her wallet, which is make-believe cow hair, but not real cowhide. "Let me pay you now."

"Okay." Matthew is glad that she isn't making him pay for the cow or the cologne.

She hands him money for the mowing and then money for baby-sitting.

Matthew looks at it and then makes a decision. "Take back the money for baby-sitting. That was an emergency and I want to help out."

Mrs. Levy gives him a great big smile and shakes her head. "Thank you. You're very nice. You worked hard. So I want to pay you."

Matthew smiles back and thinks about how good it was to make the offer and that it's also nice to still get the money.

He realizes that even if she had taken the baby-sitting money back, it would have been okay.

Leaving the house, he can hear Theo singing, "The worms crawl in, the worms crawl out," and he can hear Mrs. Levy saying, "Who taught you that?"

Matthew also realizes that as much as he needs money, baby-sitting is not going to be the way he's going to earn it.

Chapter 7

Matthew Martin, Computer Genius, Matthew thinks as he sits in front of the terminal creating a card for Jil!.

The person who I miss is Jil!
I would fone but I'm afraid of the bil!,
I like her better than pickles, sweet or dil!,
My heart, with major like, she does fil!,
If I were a fish, instead of my heart it would be my gil!,
It's really Matthew and Jill, who went up the hill,

Thinking of how far away you are makes me il!,
I'm tired of having so much time to kil!,
I'm so glad that your name is not Lil!,
I can't think of a sentence for mil!,
I'm not sure if you spell this word nil!
Vanessa Singer is still acting like a pil!,
And I want to jab her with a quil!,
I wish that you were in Califon stil!,
(the still like in "still here" not the still that makes
illegal alcohol where people pay and put money
in the til!)
If your parents let you come back soon, I will
remember
them in my wil!

Matthew pushes the print button and the card comes out.

Pleased with it, he only wishes that he already had the new program. Then he could create something really special.

There's a knock on the bedroom door, actually five knocks, followed by two more—*dum, dum, di, dum, dum . . . dum dum*—followed by Joshua calling out, "Ready or not, here I come."

The door opens.

Joshua jumps in, pretends to trip, and crumples to the floor, calling out, "I've fallen and I can't get up."

Matthew looks at his best friend and says, "You've been watching too much television."

Paula Danziger

Joshua continues to lie on the floor.

Every few minutes he attempts to rise and then slumps down again, saying, in an ever-weakening voice, "I've fallen and I can't get up."

Matthew steps over his friend and says, "Let's get going. We've got work to do."

Joshua crawls over to the computer area to see Matthew's latest project.

Jumping up, he grabs the card that is lying on the table.

Matthew rushes over to stop him but it is too late.

Joshua starts reading it aloud and laughing.

"Come on. Stop that." Matthew tries to get the card out of Joshua's hands but can't get to him because Joshua keeps jumping away from him, like a kangaroo.

"Why don't you just fall down again and not be able to get up?" Matthew tries to trip him.

Joshua jumps over Matthew's foot and exclaims, "Jil!iet, oh, Jil!iet, where fort art thou?"

"That's 'forth,' as in 'Where forth are you?' And it was Romeo, not Juliet. And that's 'forth,' like 'You're acting like a forth grader.' F-O-R-T-H." Matthew laughs. "Don't you remember anything about Shakespeare's plays after the unit Mrs. Stanton taught us?"

It's Joshua's turn to laugh. "The grade is F-O-U-R-T-H. You are the worst speller in the world."

"Thank you. Thank you." Matthew bows and then grabs the card from Joshua.

"Whatever happened to the Matthew who hated

50

girls, who wanted nothing to do with them?" Joshua teases. "The Matthew who started G.E.T.T.H.E.M.—Girls Easy to Torment Hopes Eager Matthew?"

Matthew shrugs.

He's not sure he can explain it.

He's not sure he even understands it.

Joshua continues. "Matthew, who got girls so angry that they started a group called G.E.T.H.I.M, Girls Eager to Halt Immature Matthew? And now girls like him, not just Jil! either? That new girl, Lacey, the one who is just visiting her aunt for the summer, keeps hanging around you. Do you like her?"

"Yeah. She's nice." Matthew shrugs.

"I mean, do you really like her?" Joshua looks embarrassed.

"No, not like Jil!, if that's what you mean." Matthew shakes his head. "Lacey's okay. We're just becoming friends. She just likes to talk to me."

"Yeah. Sure." Joshua doesn't look pleased.

"Look. Lacey just came to the rec center two days ago." Matthew decides to tell Joshua what Lacey has been saying, even though he promised her that he wouldn't. "Actually, the only reason that she talks to me is because you're my best friend and she wants to find out all about you."

"No." Joshua stares at Matthew. "Are you kidding me?"

Matthew raises his hand. "I swear. She's always talking about you, asking me questions like do you have a girlfriend?, do you like blondes?, what are your hobbies?''

"Really?" Joshua tries to act nonchalant. "And what did you tell her?"

"I told her that you hate most girls, think that blondes are the most disgusting people in the world, and that your hobbies are taking pictures of warts and counting people's nose hair."

Joshua bangs his head against the wall.

"Just joking." Matthew stands next to him. "I told her that at the moment you don't have a girlfriend. I didn't tell her the truth, that at no moment have you ever had a girlfriend. I told her that you like girls with blond hair and that I can tell that you like her."

"How can you tell?" Joshua challenges his friend.

Matthew laughs. "I can tell because you punch her on the arm and yesterday you went up to her and showed her your special talent, how you can take your tongue and stick it all the way up your nose."

Joshua bangs his head on the wall again. "I can't believe I did that. It was so dumb. I just wanted to walk up to her and ask her if she was going on the bowling trip, and instead I showed her that dumb trick."

Matthew pulls Joshua away from the wall. "It could have been worse. You could have stuck your tongue up *her* nose."

Joshua starts laughing. "That's so gross."

"I know. Thank you. Thank you. Thank you."

Matthew bows as if he has just received the highest compliment in the world.

Joshua decides that it's time to change the subject before Matthew really decides to start teasing him about Lacey.

He picks up the computer card that Matthew has made for Jil! and waves it in front of his friend, teasing before he can be teased. "Jil!iet, oh, Jil!iet, Where fort art thou?"

Matthew tries to grab it and trips Joshua, who, falling to the floor, grabs Matthew's leg, pulling him down.

The boys jump up and run around again.

Mrs. Martin walks into the room, her hands on her hips. "What do you think, that we live in a gymnasium?"

Joshua and Matthew pretend to be sumo wrestlers.

Mrs. Martin looks at the two boys and thinks about how the summer is just beginning and she says, "I want the two of you to go outside and play."

"We're practically seventh graders." Matthew stands up next to his mother and realizes that he's almost taller than she is. "Seventh graders don't play. We just hang out."

Joshua gets up too. "Play? We have other plans."

Matthew and Joshua exchange looks.

They've almost forgotten.

Work.

They have figured out a way to earn money.

Joshua wants a new skateboard.

Matthew wants his program.
Now if only their plan works.
Only time will tell.
And no one, they hope, will tell their parents.

Chapter 8

"Hey, mister, do you want your windshield wiped?" Matthew goes up to a car waiting at the traffic light.

The man smiles and says, "Sure."

Matthew uses a squeegee to get the window clean and then asks the man if he wants to also buy an air freshener, lemon, cherry, or pine scented, to hang from his inside car mirror.

He wants a pine-scented one.

Pocketing the money, Matthew thinks about the

number of people who pay them something for doing their windows and about how he and Joshua sold some old comic books and bought a whole box of air fresheners to hang in cars and how they are selling them for about double what they paid for them.

The light changes.

Matthew and Joshua go to the other part of the intersection, where there are cars waiting for the light to turn green.

The first car that Matthew walks up to is driven by a man who obviously is not interested.

He has turned on the windshield wipers, motioning with his hands to not go near the car and saying, "I have to deal with this every day when I commute into New York. I don't expect to have to do this in Califon, New Jersey. I moved out here to get away from all of that."

The light changes again and it's back to the other side.

Matthew and Joshua keep working, making money and thinking about their future purchases.

Matthew starts to think about how maybe they can start selling franchises, having other kids all over the country doing this and selling a special kind of air fresheners, a product, using both of their last names, called Martin Jackson. The scents could be odors like popcorn, favorite ice cream flavors, and brownie mix as it bakes. For people like his mother they can be granola and sprout scented.

A car pulls up.

It's Mrs. Stanton, his favorite teacher ever.

She pulls her car over to the side of the road and gets out.

Matthew rushes over.

So does Joshua.

While they are standing on the sidewalk, cars whiz by.

Matthew looks at them and thinks about how much money they are losing, but then thinks about how good it is to see Mrs. Stanton again, even though school has just ended.

Matthew gets right to the point and asks the question that many of their classmates want to ask. "Are you going out with Ryma's father? Are you going to marry him?"

Mrs. Stanton looks at him. "Matthew Martin. Do I ask you personal questions like that?"

"Ask him if he's going to marry Jill!" Joshua suggests.

"Ask Joshua if he's going to marry Lacey." Matthew steps on Joshua's foot and then says, "I just think that it's a good idea. Mr. Browne is really nice, and so are you. And your daughter, Marie, and Ryma are really nice. And Ryma is not in your classroom anymore, so it wouldn't be what my dad calls a 'conflict of interests.' And some of my mom's friends, who aren't married, are always saying stuff like 'There just aren't a lot of good men around.' And Mr. Browne is a good man, right? And as my grandmother says about people, 'You're not getting any younger.' So I think you ought to marry him. And when I see him, I could tell him the same thing, because he's not getting any younger either."

"Matthew . . ." is all that Mrs. Stanton manages to say before Matthew starts talking again.

"And I think it would be nice for Ryma and Marie to be sisters, since they are 'only children.' It's nice to have other kids in the family—except in my case, where my sister is a dirt ball."

"Matthew"—Mrs. Stanton stops him—"enough. I know you care about me, but my relationship with Mr. Browne is really something that I don't care to discuss."

Matthew looks confused. "Did I say anything bad?"

She smiles at him. "Not bad. Maybe a little nosy, but not bad."

He grins at her. "Well, if you do get married, can I have a piece of the wedding cake?"

She sighs and nods. "Look, boys, I didn't pull off the road to discuss my social life. I did it because I'm very concerned about what you are doing. Even though Califon is a very safe place, it's not a good idea to be going up to all of these cars and talking to strangers, walking around in the middle of traffic that may suddenly start moving, and smelling gas fumes."

"We won't get into the car," Joshua says. "And we're strong. No one can hurt us."

Mrs. Stanton shakes her head. "You know, a lot of kids think that nothing can hurt them, that nothing can happen to them. You have to be careful. I don't want to scare you from having adventures, from trying out new things, but you have to use your common sense. It's really not a smart idea to be doing this."

"But we're making money. I need it to buy a computer program. You know how you're always saying that we should learn new things," Matthew defends himself, and watches as cars filled with potential buyers of air fresheners whiz by.

She continues. "There are lots of other things that you can do to earn money."

Remembering baby-sitting for the Levy kids, Matthew says, "But this one is so easy. And really, nothing bad has happened."

"I'm only telling you this for your own good." Mrs. Stanton looks at both of the boys. "I don't want to lecture you, but I really care and don't want to see anything happen to you. I want you to understand. I want you to be responsible and careful."

Matthew hates it when grown-ups say they're only telling him something for his own good, especially when he realizes that maybe they are right.

Looking at the cars, totaling up in his head how much more he can make in a couple of hours, and figuring out how much he and Joshua spent on the box of air fresheners, he makes a decision. "We'll just finish doing this today, and then we'll find another way to make money. Please, promise that you won't tell on us to our parents."

Mrs. Stanton sighs again. She thinks about how

much easier it would have been for her if she hadn't decided to go shopping that afternoon, if she taught in a town where she didn't live.

"Please. Don't tell them." Matthew puts his palms together and begs her.

Before she has a chance to answer, another car pulls up behind hers.

It's Mr. Jackson, who has just been called by a neighbor who saw the boys doing windows.

Mr. Jackson does not look very happy.

Chapter 9

I'm in deep doo-doo. Very deep doo-doo, Matthew thinks as he sits down on the living-room couch.

His father is sitting on the recliner to the right of the couch.

His mother is sitting on the rocker to the left of the couch.

Looking from right to left, from left to right, Matthew thinks, *Oh, great. This is going to be in stereo . . . a parent on each side yelling at me.*

From the frowns on their faces, their eyes narrowed to tiny slits, and their arms crossed in front of them, Matthew realizes that his parents are not going to go easy on him.

One of the things that is really making him nervous is that his parents hardly ever yell at him, hardly ever punish him, and have never believed in spanking. He's not sure of what they are going to do in this situation.

Another thing that is making him nervous is that his father is a lawyer and is really good at handling criminals, although Matthew is not quite sure of how big a "crime" they think he's committed.

He also feels bad because he has been trying so hard to be more grown up, to make them see that he is no longer a child.

"Matthew," his father says in his deep, serious voice, "we want to give you a few minutes to think about why we are here having this discussion, about what you have done that concerns us."

For a minute Matthew considers saying, *We're here because it's more comfortable for discussions and family meetings than, say, the bathroom.*

He decides not to open his mouth.

Mrs. Martin frowns. "We want you to think about this seriously, not try to get out of it by making jokes, trying to be cute."

Rats, Matthew thinks. *Cute is usually the thing that works best on her.*

"Think, Matthew, think. And then be prepared to discuss this." Mr. Martin has the recliner straight up, a sure sign that there is not going to be any relaxation for a while.

His parents say nothing for a few minutes and then start giving all the reasons that they are upset by what he has done.

Matthew has heard the same things from Mrs. Stanton, Mr. Jackson, and now his parents.

Matthew, who has perfected the art of looking at people as if he is paying perfect attention, stares intently at his parents and starts to think about other things. *This is all Amanda's fault. If she hadn't gone away to camp, they would be spending all of their time worrying about her, disciplining her. This is all Joshua's fault. If he didn't have a father who was a free-lance writer, no one would have been home to get the call from the busybody who told on us. This is all the computer company's fault. If they didn't charge so much, I wouldn't have had to try so hard to earn the money. This is all my parents' fault. They make money. They should be willing to share it with their kids.*

Matthew thinks about how it's not fair to torture a kid like this—to keep lecturing him when all he tried to do was earn some money for an educational and fun computer program.

He recalls how Mr. Jackson yelled at them and, when he dropped Matthew off at his house, ordered him in the name of his parents to go directly to his room. He made Matthew promise to stay there until his parents came home, not to use his computer, not to watch television, not to use the phone, except to call his parents, whom Mr. Jackson had spoken to from his car phone.

It was torture for Matthew to wait, to not know what his parents were going to say.

It was such torture, so nerve racking, so boring just waiting, that he actually cleaned up his room, an act that he hoped would make his parents less angry at him. An act that also yielded four quarters, two dimes, seventeen nickels, and one hundred thirty-two pennies —three dollars thirty-seven cents toward the new program.

But Matthew can't stand it much longer.

He can't stand thinking about what he did, what's going to happen next.

Wishing that it was already a half an hour in the future, he bites his bottom lip and speaks up as soon as his parents finish with their concerns. "Look. I didn't mean to do anything wrong. You knew that I was going to try to earn some money, and I did. I didn't do anything illegal. Don't you believe in free enterprise?"

"Bad argument," Matthew's father says.

So I want to be a computer programmer, not a lawyer, Matthew thinks, getting a little angry but afraid to say it out loud.

His father continues, "If you thought that it was all right to do this, why didn't you tell us?"

"We didn't think it was going to be such a big deal, honest." Matthew looks first at his father, then at his mother. "It was just a way to earn money."

"You should have told us," Mrs. Martin says.

Matthew decides to try to make his parents feel as guilty as they're making him feel. "I would have, but you are always at work, always too busy."

There's a gasp from his mother. "Matthew Martin. I didn't go into work until late today. Someone else was watching the store. We had time enough to discuss Shakespeare's plays this morning. We would have had time enough to talk about your business idea."

Matthew's not ready to give up trying to make his parents feel guilty. "If you had just bought the program for me, this would have never happened."

His parents exchange looks.

Mr. Martin speaks. "Matthew, you and Josh could have been hurt . . . or worse. That's the issue here. Didn't you boys think about the risk?"

"No." Matthew is adamant. "We didn't. Joshua and I were watching television and we saw a show where people did it and we thought we should try. We really, honestly, truly, just thought that was a good way to earn money. And it was."

His parents exchange looks again.

"Okay, Matthew. We're willing to believe you, but can you see why we're so concerned?" His mother rocks back and forth on her chair.

Matthew thinks about it. All of the stuff that Mrs. Stanton said, all the reasons Mr. Jackson gave, his parents' concerns.

He thinks. It was really easy money. It also was a little dangerous. The gas fumes made him cough. Joshua really had to jump once to get out of the way of

a car that was trying to run the light. Matthew decides
to give in on this one but hopes that he can come up
with another way to make money.

He gives in, not happily, but he does relent.
"Okay. So it was dumb. I'm sorry. I won't do it again."

"Good. And you'll talk to us before you do something to earn money," his mother continues.

Matthew nods again. "Okay. Is there a time limit
on this rule, though? Is there ever going to be a time
I'm old enough to pick my own job?"

"Don't get smart, young man." His father shakes
his finger. "You're only eleven years old and we want
to help you to do the best."

"I'm going to be twelve soon," Matthew reminds
them.

"When you're twelve, we're still going to be offering advice and, at times, telling you what you have to
do," his father informs him.

"Matthew, when you are forty-one, almost forty-
two, we'll probably still be offering advice, trying to
guide you," his mother tells him.

"Am I going to be punished?" Matthew can't
stand the suspense anymore.

"Do you think you should be?" his father asks.

Matthew shakes his head. "No. Absolutely, posi-
tively not. I think that this is what you call a 'learning
experience' and I've learned and shouldn't have to be
punished."

There's silence, and then . . .

"We agree," his mother says.

"Whew." Matthew takes a deep breath.

"There is something that we want you to know." His father leans forward. "We've talked with Joshua's parents and we don't want you boys to keep the money that you've earned."

"Oh, no." Matthew sinks back into the sofa cushions and lets what his parents have just told him sink into his brain. "Not a cent?"

"Not a cent," they repeat.

If this isn't a punishment, Matthew is not sure what it is.

"Can't we even get back the money that Joshua and I paid for the box of air fresheners?" Matthew begs.

"You can get that back, but the profits you boys will give to charity."

Matthew scrunches his nose. "How about fifty percent to charity and fifty percent to us?"

"Not negotiable," his father says. "You and Joshua will pick out a charity and donate the money to it."

Defeated, Matthew thinks about which charity to choose.

He decides. "I know. We'll give the money to the charity that helps out the homeless in New York, especially the people who wash windshields."

"Good." His mother comes over to the sofa, sits down, and hugs him.

Matthew debates telling her that he is getting too old for hugs, at least ones from his mother, but decides not to, since he really likes the hug, especially now.

His father says, "We have another matter we want to discuss with you."

Matthew goes through a list of things in his head that his parents might want to lecture him about—his normally cluttered room, the chocolate bars that he keeps hidden in his underwear drawer, his new interest in girls. He decides that's it. They are going to give him the big talk, the one about birds and bees. The one about S-E-X.

Mrs. Martin stops hugging him and puts her hands on his shoulders. "Your father and I have decided to tell you something very important and very personal."

This is it, Matthew guesses.

And he waits expectantly for the Big Talk to begin.

Chapter 10

Mrs. Martin speaks first. "You may have wondered why your father and I aren't buying you the computer program. We want to explain."

Matthew's a little confused. *Is there*, he wonders, *a computer program for sale that teaches people about the facts of life?* He thinks about how that really gives new meaning to the term *user friendly*. He wonders if the person operates a keyboard or mouse to get all the answers, to get all the information shown on the computer. Matthew wonders what the graphics would be like for that program.

"Matthew, back to earth. This is important," his father says. "Your mother and I want to explain to you why we want you to earn part of the money for the computer program, the one that we've agreed to share the cost of."

Oops, not the S-E-X lecture, Matthew figures out. He is very disappointed, and at the same time a little relieved.

Mrs. Martin looks at her son. "When your father and I first got married . . ."

Well, maybe, he thinks.

She continues, "We were just starting out and didn't have very much money, so we got into very bad habits. We borrowed money against our future earnings. We charged far too much on credit cards. We spent more than we made."

Matthew starts thinking about what his parents are really talking about and he starts to get very worried. "You don't do that now, do you?"

"No." Mr. Martin takes over. "We don't. We cut up all of our credit cards, except for the ones we use for business. We worked out a repayment schedule and a budget. It took a long time but everything got straightened out."

Mrs. Martin holds on to her son's hand. "Matthew, honey, Dad just made it sound very easy . . . but it wasn't. There were times when we were afraid to pick up the phone, that there would be yet another creditor on the line."

"It was like a juggling act—rent, phone, food, clothes, charge cards, paying back loans from our parents, college loans." Mr. Martin has a very pained look on his face.

Mrs. Martin looks very sad.

Mr. Martin gets up and joins his wife and son on the couch. "We were young, just out of college. It was the first time that we had our own money—two salaries, no kids—and we bought all sorts of things. A car . . . new furniture. We went for immediate gratification, meaning if we saw it and wanted it, we bought it, even if we didn't have the money saved. Lots of companies gave us credit and we used it. And then, it just got to the point where we were totally out of control."

Matthew is amazed. He's always thought that his parents could handle just about anything, that they never had any problems. He hardly ever thinks about the fact that they even had a life before he was born.

"It was a terrible time. We had to go to a special agency that helps out people who are in that kind of trouble. They made us cut up our cards. They contacted all our creditors, got them to accept less money over a longer period of time. We had to live on a very strict budget."

"We used to have pasta almost every night because it was so cheap." His father wipes the tears off his wife's face with a handkerchief.

71

She begins to smile, remembering. "The only good thing was that we couldn't afford to buy junk food."

"That was one of the really bad things," his father remembers.

Mrs. Martin shakes her head quickly, as if trying to toss all the bad memories out. "So you see why we worry about you. You're doing some of the same things that we did. When you want something, you have to have it immediately, even if you can't afford it. You never plan ahead, never save any money. You get advances on your allowance that you never manage to pay back. You owe money to a lot of people. It makes us very nervous. We know that sometimes we confuse you because we buy a lot for you and your sister. But we want you to know that there are limits. So now you know, and we want all of us to work on this problem before it overwhelms you."

Matthew feels overwhelmed by what they have just told him. "Maybe someday I can win the lottery. Then I won't have to worry about all of this. I'll win so much that I can have whatever I want."

"This is not going to be easy." Mrs. Martin sighs, then continues, "Look, Matthew, we *earn* our money. We don't expect a magical solution."

Rats, Matthew thinks.

Mrs. Martin says, "We have savings and no longer overspend. We're able to meet our needs and buy some luxuries. But we do know what really counts. And we consider ourselves very lucky. Look at all the people in the world who don't even have the basic necessities."

Matthew is getting a headache, hearing more than he wants to hear. His parents have made major mistakes. He has yet another possible growing-up problem. His very own parents sometimes had trouble handling grown-up things when they were grown-ups. Clearly this having to handle money in an adult way is not a one-shot deal.

He wishes he never had to deal with all of this stuff, and he begins to realize that he's not even going to have a choice about whether or not he can deal with this issue. He's going to have to do it no matter what.

"Rats," he says. "Now I really understand why Peter Pan never wanted to grow up."

His father nods. "Once I tried calling up AAA, The American Automobile Association—the group that helps members plan trips—and asked them for the road map to never-never land."

Matthew laughs.

"It's true. He really did it," his mother informs him.

"And?" Matthew wants the details. "Let me guess what they told you, that there was no way to get there from here."

"And," his father says, "they told me that there was no way to get there from here."

Matthew knows that he doesn't want to deal with all of this money stuff—not even for a billion gazillion dollars. He also knows that he has no choice.

Chapter 11

Dear Matthew,
I miss you!!!!!//!!!!!
I wish I were back
in Califon!!!!
There's been a chemical
spill so we can't swim in
the lake.
My darling brother (HA) has
poison ivy all over his bratty
body. (He took off all his clothes
and rolled around in a pile of leaves)
My Mom is very pregnant, HOT,
GRUMPY, & sure she is going to
give birth to a water Buffalo!
I miss you.
LOVE, JIL! XXXXXX XXXXX XXXXXXXXXX

MATTHEW
MARTIN
School St.
Califon, N.J.
07830

Matthew puts the postcard back in his pocket and
thinks about how much he misses Jil!, how he doesn't
really understand this whole boyfriend-girlfriend
thing, but he knows that he really likes her a lot.

If Jil! were here, he could talk to her about all the
stuff that's going on . . . how his parents made him
write down a list of everyone he owed money to . . .
how they loaned him the money to pay off his debts,
and how he now has to pay them back by getting only

fifty percent of his allowance until the debt clears. If Jil! were here, he would have someone to hang out with who really liked his sense of humor, someone who thought he was really special.

If Jil! were here, he would have to pay her the money that he owes her, money that he forgot to put on the list.

But Jil!'s not here, he thinks, and walks over to the recreation field.

As he walks past the bleachers, he can see a high-school couple, who are not part of the town recreational program, kissing. Matthew guesses that they have their own recreational program.

Eddie, the head counselor, goes over to the bleachers to tell them to stop.

Matthew thinks about Jil! and wonders whether they would be kissing on the bleachers if she hadn't gone away. He decides that they probably wouldn't, that they would be hanging out with the rest of their friends. He thinks much more about kissing than actually doing it.

Looking around, Matthew can see that the rec field is filled.

The nine–ten-year-old group is lined up by the pool, getting partners, having their names put up on the buddy board to be sure that they all stay safe and accounted for.

Walter Carlson is swatting girls' rear ends with his towel.

Anita Mastripoli gives Walter a karate chop.

Their counselors separate them.

Playing dodge ball, the five- and six-year-olds are screaming loudly as they either try to duck from or hit each other with a huge foam ball.

One of the little boys is hiding out behind a garbage can, trying not to get hit and picking his nose.

It reminds Matthew of one of his favorite jokes:

Q. What's the difference between snot and broccoli?

A. Kids won't eat broccoli.

Matthew continues walking across the playground, passing by the group of seven- and eight-year-olds, on the equipment that the people of the town designed and built.

Matthew finds his group in the arts-and-crafts building.

As he enters, he notices that Joshua is standing next to the bench where Lacey is decorating a sweatshirt with puff paints and glitter.

Matthew debates asking Joshua since when has he become so interested in the puff paint and glitter movement in American art but decides not to embarrass him, at least not in front of everyone else.

Vanessa Singer holds her nose and says, "Fe, fi, fo, fum, I smell the smell of a dum-dum."

Matthew turns to her. "You wouldn't if you learned to use deodorant."

"A point for Matthew." Joshua licks his finger and keeps score on the air.

"Unnecessary. This squabbling is so unnecessary."

Susie Gifford, the arts-and-crafts counselor, looks up from the T-shirt she is helping Cathy Atwood fix after an unfortunate spill of puff paint and glitter.

"It is so necessary," Matthew explains. "Squabbling with Vanessa is my hobby."

Vanessa glares at Matthew. "Two years ago I made a list of rotten things to say to Matthew, and I'm only halfway through them."

"Susie, just give up any thoughts of them getting along." Lisa scratches a mosquito bite and leaves a patch of pink puff paint and glitter on her face. "We're all used to it. If someone ever wrote a story about those two, it would end, AND THEY FOUGHT HAPPILY EVER AFTER."

"I'm majoring in psychology. They could be my case study." Susie tries to wipe the mess off Lisa's face.

"No problem," Vanessa explains. "We just don't like each other. We abhor each other, detest each other."

"We have allergic reactions to each other, have contempt for each other," Matthew elaborates.

Susie thinks about changing her major to something like forestry.

Lisa decides to change the subject. "Who's going on the camp bowling trip?"

Most of the kids look at each other to make sure that others look like they're going before raising their hands.

Tyler and Zoe are the first to raise their hand—

actually hands—but since they are always holding each other's, it looks like one hand.

Everyone else raises his or her hand, except for Matthew, who with his reduced allowance has to figure out if he's going on the trip or going to the movies this week.

Finally, he raises his hand.

"Rats," Vanessa says.

"Why are you calling for your family?" Matthew asks, and then turns to the rest of the group, ignoring Vanessa. "So what are we making in here?"

"Glitter T-shirts." Ryma holds hers up. On the left side she has drawn a glitter pink puffed heart.

"What are the guys doing?" Matthew has no desire to work with glitter and puff paint.

"Watching the girls make these dorky things and hanging out talking to them," Billy Kellerman informs him. "The counselors won't let us use the basketball courts now because the little kids are using them, and they say we pick on them and don't give them a chance to play."

"Us?" Mark laughs. "Would we do a thing like that?"

All of the boys think about how when they were little, the big guys did that to them and now it is their turn—not to torment the younger kids, but just to let them know who's boss.

Matthew and Joshua go over to the side of the room and sit alone at a table.

"Did your parents yell a lot?" Matthew asks.

Joshua shakes his head. "No. They just said that they, and your parents, decided that we had to give the money we *earned* to charity."

"Bummer." Matthew pulls at a splinter on the table. "I really could have used the money."

"Me too." Joshua envisions the skateboard that he would have bought.

"What are we going to do with the rest of the air fresheners?" Matthew makes a face. "We're stuck with a lot of those suckers."

"At least our parents let us keep the money we spent on them." Reminding him, Josh takes off his baseball cap and puts it on backwards. "So even though we're stuck with them, we didn't lose the money, since we sold enough of them at double what they cost us."

"Maybe we should sell them door to door." Matthew has visions of being ninety years old before he gets the computer program.

"Fat chance." Joshua punches him on the arm. "You doofus, do you really think that our parents will let us do that? They'll say that we could get killed by an ax murderer."

"But we know practically everyone in our neighborhood," Matthew argues.

"I know our parents," Joshua says. "They'll say that we could be killed by a *visiting* ax murderer."

Matthew shrugs. "Well, I'm going to ask my parents if it's okay. If it's not, maybe we can sell the air fresheners for kids to put on bikes, or sell a pair as earrings. . . ."

Joshua looks at him as if he's gone off the deep end.

Even Matthew realizes how silly it sounds, but he really wants to buy the program.

Zoe walks up. "I spoke to Jil! last night. She really liked the card you sent her. I think the things that you wrote are really sweet."

Blushing, Matthew can't believe that Jil! read it to Zoe, Califon's own answer to the Pony Express Information Service.

"She said that it arrived a little rumpled," Zoe informs him. "She said it looked like someone had been using it in a game of keep-away."

Matthew and Joshua look at each other and think about how the game was more like "Where Fort Art Thou."

Zoe continues speaking, putting her head on Tyler's shoulder. "Even though my Tyler is a practically perfect boyfriend, I wish that he would send me a card like that. Jil! is sooooo lucky."

Matthew blushes again.

"What does the card say?" Billy Kellerman jumps into the conversation, hoping to find out something to tease Matthew about.

Zoe shrugs. "I'm not sure I remember. After all, it wasn't about me. But I remember thinking that I wished Tyler would do something like that for me, using *my* name."

Getting up to go to the girls' room, one of the few places that she doesn't go with Tyler, Zoe repeats, "It would be so wonderful if my Tyler did that for me."

Zoe goes out of the room.

Once everyone is sure that she is out of hearing range, the comments start.

"Oh, Tylerpoo, please write something for me!" Billy uses a high-pitched voice.

"Well, Tyler, if you want her still to think you're perfect you better write a card just as wonderful as Matthew's. You know Zoe when she decides she wants something." Cathy puts a rhinestone on her creation.

Matthew thinks about how hard it would be to do a poem that rhymed with Zoe—Zoe E.

He decides that the only way to make it work would be to make believe that every rhyme ended with O E.

Thinking for a minute, he finally says,

"There once was a girl named Zoe,
Who in a blender stuck her Toe,
She cried out E I E I O E,
Tyler came along and pulled it out with a Hoe,
Now she's out of Woe,
And glad that she goes out with Tyler instead of some guy named Joey."

"That is so lame." Brian laughs.

"I like it," Tyler says, flexing his muscles. "It shows what a hero I am."

Someone at the girls' table starts making retching sounds.

"Would you make up a computer card for me?" Tyler turns to Matthew. "You know, write it up, adding pictures like you always do."

Matthew thinks about how much time it will take.

Joshua steps up to Tyler. "How much are you willing to pay him? I'm his business manager."

Matthew looks at his friend and realizes once more why he is glad that Joshua Jackson is his best friend.

"You can do it yourself. It's a piece of cake," Vanessa tells Tyler.

Matthew looks at her and realizes once more why Vanessa Singer is his worst enemy.

"Not as well as Matthew can," Tyler decides.

The boys settle on a price for the card before Zoe returns.

Matthew and Joshua exchange glances.

A new business is about to start, one that won't upset their parents.

Matthew Martin is one happy person.

He can't imagine what else could happen to make the day any better.

And then Jil! walks in the door.

Chapter 12

Everyone starts talking at once.

Everyone except for Matthew, who sits there very quietly, very glad to see Jil!, but not very sure of how to react in front of everyone else, not very sure of how to act to Jil!.

The questions come all at once.

"When did you get back?"

"How long are you staying?"

"Where did you get that outfit? Can I borrow it sometime?"

"Are you going on the bowling trip later this week?"

"Is something the matter? Is your mom okay?"

"How come you didn't tell me when we talked on the phone that you were coming back so soon?" Zoe has walked back into the arts-and-crafts room. "Did you miss Matthew so much that you ran away from the lake and returned here to be with him?"

Everyone looks at Zoe and starts to laugh.

She is offended by their reactions. "Well, it could happen. Something like that just happened on my favorite soap opera—and anyway, something like that happened with my mother and one of her husbands."

People stop laughing, because they know that Zoe's life is so much like a soap opera, with her parents' many marriages and divorces, that she expects just about anything to be possible.

Jil! starts answering the questions. "We got back about an hour ago. Actually, we weren't expecting to come back at all, but my mother said she couldn't stand seeing my father only weekends. He couldn't commute to work from the lake, and we couldn't use it because it was polluted by some dumb factory. It was so depressing watching all the dead fish floating on top of the water. And then my stupid little brother got poison ivy all over his stupid little body and spent the entire time sitting nude in the house, covered with calamine lotion, whimpering in his stupid little voice. And although I did try to be a saint about the whole situation, I guess I did complain just a little bit, about how much I missed all of you, about how much I missed being in Califon, how there was no one at the lake to hang out with, about how my stupid little brother and his stupid little whining was driving me crazy. So my mother, who as you all know is going to give birth sometime in September, decided to return to Califon."

"Boy. She's only been gone a week and I forgot how dramatic she is." Billy strikes a pose. "Ask her a question and you get a three-act play."

Jil! slugs him in the arm.

And then she looks at Matthew.

He looks back, feeling a little shy in front of all their friends.

"So is that a new outfit?" Cathy asks. "It sure would look good on me."

"Why don't you try it on right now?" David asks. "You could change right here right now."

Cathy picks up the jar of glitter and sprinkles some of it on his head.

"You have to excuse him." Joshua laughs. "He's been like this since his brothers started sharing their copies of *Playboy* with him."

"There is no excuse for him." Cathy pours a different-color glitter on him, glad that the counselor has stepped out for a break so that she isn't there to yell for wasting materials.

Matthew thinks about how one of David's older brothers used to go out with his sister, Amanda. He's sure that Danny didn't go out with Amanda because

Paula Danziger

she looks like a *Playboy* centerfold. The only resemblance, he thinks, is that the paper it's printed on is flat and so is Amanda.

He wonders for a minute how Amanda is doing at camp and he thinks about how quiet it is in the house without her.

He looks at Jil!, who is looking at him.

Wondering if he is supposed to say something to David because of his comments, he decides not to.

Instead, he stands up and says, "I'm thirsty and am going to the fountain for some water. Want to come with me, Jil!?"

"Ooooow . . ."

"How can she ever turn down an offer like that?"

"How romantic."

Jil! stands up and curtsies. "Why, sir, I thought you'd never ask."

As they walk out of the arts-and-crafts area, they can hear some of the boys making kissing sounds on their hands and some of the girls saying, "You are soooooooooooooo immature."

Matthew looks at Jil!.

Jil! looks at Matthew.

Neither is sure of what to say or do.

But they are very glad to see each other.

As they walk past the nine–ten-year-old group, they can hear them singing,

"Everyone's doing it . . .
Doing it . . .

86

Picking their nose and chewing it,
Chewing it,
They think it's candy . . .
But it's . . . snot."

Jil! looks at Matthew. "That song is so disgusting."
Matthew, who really likes the song, just smiles.

Reaching the water fountain, Matthew, still not at all sure of how to act when you have a girlfriend, lets Jil! get the first drink of water and resists the temptation while she is sipping to push her head into the fountain, which is what he would have done a few months earlier.

It's his turn and he bends down to sip the water.

Jil! pushes his head into the fountain.

Lifting his dripping wet head, Matthew looks at Jil! and says, "Welcome back."

Chapter 13

"This meeting is now called to order." Matthew raps on the desk in his father's study. Since he does not have a gavel, he uses the four-foot-tall purple crayon that usually leans against the wall.

"Order. I'll order a hot pastrami on rye." Joshua raises his hand. "And a root-beer float."

That reminds Matthew. "Did you bring any junk food from your houses?"

"Brownies that my dad baked." Joshua holds up a bag.

Jil! also holds up a bag. "I got M&M's, Mallomars, and chocolate-covered prunes."

"Ugh" is the response from the boys about her third offering.

"Chocolate-covered prunes. You don't even want to know the disgusting things I'm thinking about that." Matthew grimaces. "Where did they come from?"

"From chocolate-covered plums." Joshua laughs.

Jil! shrugs. "My mother has these strange cravings when she's pregnant."

Matthew, a person who will eat almost anything that has chocolate, realizes that he has finally found something he will not taste.

He raps on the table again. "I move that we eat the Mallomars now and then discuss our company. All in favor, say aye. All opposed, give their cookies to me."

There are three ayes.

Eating the cookies, the three friends start discussing the company they are starting.

Everyone will be equal, get an equal share of the profits.

Matthew will be in charge of developing, designing, and producing the products that come out of the computer.

Joshua will be the publicity and promotion person, the one who oversees getting business, advertising, and the distribution of the finished products.

Jil! will be in charge of keeping track of the finances—what is spent, how much goes back into the company, and how much they get. She will also help Matthew with his spelling.

"So here are the items on the agenda." Matthew licks the chocolate off the top of the Mallomar. "What are we going to name our company? What exactly are we able to do? What do we charge? And how many snack breaks do we get?"

Since there are three members of the company, the name choices start out by centering on that fact: The Three Musketeers. The Three Stooges. The Three Bears. The Three Bares (that from Joshua, who has been looking at David's copies of *Playboy*). The Three Little Kittens . . .

"Forget it." Matthew picks up another Mallomar. "How about Mart in Cards? You know, like Mart, selling . . . like Martin, my last name. I love puns, don't you?"

"Not as much as you do." Joshua grabs two Mallomars, afraid that if he doesn't get his share right away, Matthew will vacuum the rest of the cookies into his body. "Look. We're all part of the company. We could take part of each of our names and make it Martin, Jackson, and Hudson . . . two sons and a daughter."

"Not enough pizzazz." Jil! tries one of the chocolate-covered prunes and immediately spits it into her hand. "Aarg."

"Aarg is a dumb name for the company," Matthew informs her.

A quick trip to the bathroom to throw out the

chocolate mess and a fast wash of her hands, and Jil! is back. "I have it. Let's use none of our own names. Let's just make up a name. That's what all the big companies do. I bet there is no Betty Crocker, no Aunt Jemima."

"No Mac Kintosh," Matthew adds. "You know, like the guy who invented the computers."

"That's Macintosh, like the Apple, doofus." Joshua sighs.

Matthew grins.

Jil! continues. "So here's my idea. Let's call the company Ima Card, Inc. We'll leave out the skiggly line between *I* and *m* and act like Ima is the person's first name and Card is her last. And the Inc. is for Incorporated. That's all of us."

"The skiggly line is an apostrophe," Joshua informs her.

"Whatever." Jil! shrugs. "It's summer. I don't have to remember school stuff now."

Matthew runs over to the computer and types something into it. Then he puts rainbow-colored paper into the printer and pushes a button.

A banner is made—IMA CARD, INK.

Joshua and Jil! applaud and then look at the banner carefully.

"Matthew, you spell Inc. I-N-C." Joshua shakes his head.

"I like it." Jil! giggles. "It looks like we did it intentionally, since we're going to be printing things up."

The three friends stare at the banner.

Matthew thinks of a phrase he has heard his father use when he talks about things going really well.

He picks up the sign and hands one end of it to Joshua.

The middle section goes to Jil! and he holds the other end.

"This is," Matthew says, "going to be a banner year for our company."

And so the business begins.

Chapter 14

IMA CARD, INK.

DO YOU NEED:

★ specialized cards ★★ signs ★★ banners ★ ★★ letterheads ★★ certificates ★★ invitations ★★ menus ★★ address books ★★ personalized calendars (you'll never forget an important date) ★★ book markers ★★ book covers ★★ board games ★★ wallpaper ★★ wrapping paper ★★ your own comic books ★★★★★★★★★you name it — we'll do it (keep it clean, etc.)

Contact:
Matthew Martin
Jil! Hudson
Joshua Jackson
} phone # 555-9763

	Frame 1	Frame 2	Frame 3	Frame 4		
MATTHEW MARTIN	[5][4] 9	[9][/] 27	[8][1] 36	[7][2] 45		
Jill!	[5][4] 9	28	[8][1] 37	[9][/]		
(Jo)	[3][2] 5	[5][1] 11	[8][-] 19	[5][1] 25		
Tyler	[9][/] 20	[X] 40	[4][/] 59	[9][/]		
Joshua	[6][3] 9	[5][2] 16	[8][/] 33	[7][1] 41		
LACEY	[3][5] 8	[6][/] 27	[9][-]	[X]		

"Mister, is it all right for me to put this sign up on your bulletin board? Please." Matthew hands one of the Ima Card, Ink., fliers to the man behind the desk.

"Just a minute, sonny," the man says. "I have to give these two little girls their bowling shoes and then I'll be right with you. It'll just take a minute."

"Don't you have any with sparkly laces?" one of the eight-year-old girls asks.

"This is a bowling alley, not a shoe store," the man says for the eleventh time that morning, for the one thousand five hundred and forty-second time since he bought the business.

"Do I have to wear a pair of shoes with the size

printed on the back? When I wear them, my brother says that four and a half is my IQ, not my shoe size." The other girl puts her elbows up on the counter.

Matthew thinks that her older brother is probably being generous in thinking that her IQ is that high.

He is anxious, since it is almost his turn to bowl.

Shaking his head, the man says, "These are our rental shoes. Take them or leave them. Take them and you can bowl. Leave them, and unless you have your own regulation bowling shoes, you can sit on the sidelines and watch your friends bowl. It's your choice."

Looking toward the lane where his friends are bowling, Matthew hopes that the girls make a decision quickly.

Finally, they decide.

The bowling shoes go on their feet and they leave.

"At last." Matthew turns back to the man. "So would it be all right to put this up on the bulletin board?"

After the owner looks at the flier, he asks, "Is this your business?"

"Mine and my two friends'," Matthew informs him. "We're just a couple of kids trying to earn some money, keep ourselves out of trouble by printing up things that people can use." Matthew is impressed with his own explanation and hopes that the man is, also.

"So, if I let you put this up on my bulletin board, what's in it for me?" The man smiles at him.

Matthew thinks fast and smiles back. "What's in it for you, you ask? I'll tell you—our undying gratitude and we'll make up a couple of signs for you to put up on your counter. One will be THIS IS NOT A SHOE STORE. IT'S A BOWLING ALLEY. The second one will be, YOU'LL NEVER STRIKE OUT AT THE CALIFON BOWL. . . . WE HAVE BOWLING BALLS TO SPARE."

"Matthew, it's your turn," Jil! yells.

"In a second," he yells back.

He stares at the man and says, "Oh, please. . . . say yes. My friends are always telling me that I won't take care of the business stuff, that I just want to create. This will help get them off my back."

"Matthew." Joshua cups his hands and yells.

The owner says, "I'll get the two signs? Right?"

Matthew nods.

"You can put your flier up and I'll leave it there for the month." The man turns to get shoes for new customers.

"Thank you." Matthew tacks the flier on the bulletin board and returns to his friends.

He looks at the scores.

Tyler is ahead, but that's no surprise.

Tyler is always ahead in anything sportslike.

Zoe is losing because she can't manage to concentrate on anything that is not facing in the general direction of Tyler.

Matthew looks at his own score.

He's not going to win, but he's not embarrassing himself either.

Just as Matthew is ready to bowl, the little boy in the right alley drops his ball. It comes rolling over and hits Matthew's foot.

It's gutter-ball time for Matthew Martin.

Limping slightly and dramatically, Matthew moves to throw the second ball.

This time a little girl on the left alley rolls her ball and herself down the lane.

Matthew loses concentration and only gets five pins down.

As Matthew sits down on the bench, Joshua says, "Tough luck."

Matthew watches as Joshua tries to find a way to put his arm around Lacey's shoulder.

Matthew sees Joshua's arm rise slightly, then fall back, and then watches as Joshua tries to nonchalantly place his arm on the back of Lacey's seat.

Just as Joshua's arm is close to Lacey's shoulders, she gets up to bowl.

Matthew remembers how he used to be that way with Jil!.

Joshua decides to get his mind off the arm-around-the-shoulders problem and asks, "Do you think we'll get more work soon?"

"I just got a job from that kid over there." Matthew points to a six-year-old who is tripping over his shoelaces as he bowls.

"Probably not one of our bigger jobs," Joshua guesses. "We're not going to get rich from that one."

Matthew laughs. "Actually, he wants a card made

for his older sister, one of Amanda's friends. He wants it to say EAT POOP AND DIE."

"Matthew." Jil! makes a face.

"I told him we would do it for a dime. That's all he could afford. I figure younger brothers have to stick up for each other against older sisters."

"I'm an older sister with a younger brother," Jil! reminds him.

Matthew chooses to ignore her statement. "Every dime adds up."

"It will cost more than a dime to make." Jil! sighs and then says, "Oh, well."

Lacey returns and sits down.

Joshua manages to put his arm around her shoulder.

"Your turn, Joshua," Tyler calls out.

As Joshua gets up, he moves his arm, catching his wristwatch in Lacey's hair.

Both of them look like they are going to die, especially since everyone else starts laughing.

Finally Jil! helps liberate the watch.

As Josh goes up to bowl, he can be heard mumbling, "Okay, Earth. Just swallow me up right now. Do your worst."

"He's just so cute." Lacey pats her hair back into place.

Joshua bowls a strike and comes back to sit down, feeling a million times better.

Jil! says, "Business meeting in four days. On Friday."

"So soon?" Matthew hates business meetings because Jil! always wants to talk about things like budgets, costs, and effective use of time.

"So soon." Jil! hands him a piece of her candy bar.

"Oh, okay. Until then we can just have fun?" Matthew pops the piece of candy into his mouth, quickly swallows it, and then sticks a chocolate tongue out at her.

"Until then we can just have fun." She relents.

Matthew grins at her and hopes that by Friday she will forget about the meeting.

Somehow he knows that isn't going to happen.

Chapter 15

"Matthew Martin. Joshua Jackson." Jil! stamps her foot. "I want the two of you to stop playing that computer game right now."

Staring intently at the screen, Matthew says, "Just a few more minutes."

"You said that a half an hour ago." Jil! holds up some papers. "We have to hold a business meeting and discuss what we've done, what we still have to do, and how to get more business."

Matthew, who likes the creating part of the business but hates the details, keeps staring at the screen. "Rats. You made me miss."

"Finally." Joshua takes over the controls. "I thought I was never going to get another turn."

"Rats. You made me miss," Matthew repeats. "And I was sooo close to beating my own record."

"What a pity," Jil! says sarcastically. "Just because you've made almost enough to reach your goal doesn't mean that it's time to quit. We still have a lot of orders to fill and I think we should get more business. Just think of all the things we can buy and not have to beg our parents for money . . . and anyway, I think doing this has been very exciting."

"Kaboom," Joshua yells. "I just got blown away."

"My turn." Matthew takes over the controls again.

Jil! stares at the two boys and then starts mumbling, "I'm so glad that we had this little conversation. It's such a joy to be in charge of the organizational part of our business, especially when there is so much cooperation. Well, never mind about me. I'll just go sit in the other room and see what is on television and maybe bite my nails down to nothingness, while I await your presence at the meeting. Or maybe I should just sit and listen to my ulcer develop when I think of how I'm going to have to explain to our customers why their orders are not ready."

Matthew and Joshua continue to play the computer game as Jil! goes into the living room.

Finding the remote-control device, she throws herself down on the sofa and aims the control at the TV. "Zap. Take that."

The TV switches on to the station that Mr. and Mrs. Martin watch the most, the public television channel.

Jil! gets ready to change it until she notices a little girl on it, one with blond braids and blue eyes, who looks just like her cousin.

Looking closely, she quickly realizes that it is not her cousin but stays tuned anyway.

The announcer is talking about how the little girl's family lives at the poverty level.

Jil! is positive that she's not her cousin, since her aunt and uncle have a lot of money.

Matthew walks in and sits down next to Jil!. "I quit the game. I wasn't even losing. I'm sorry that I was such a doofus. I know we should be working. Joshua is still playing the game, but only until we make up and then he'll come in and join us."

"Shhhhh." Jil! puts her hand on his arm. "I want to listen to this show. It's so sad."

Matthew keeps quiet, knowing how Jil! is always interested in sad things. He remembers how every book report she did in fifth grade was about someone who was sick, dying, or dead. He remembers how in sixth grade she would get really upset when Mrs. Stanton would talk to them about some of the problems in the world.

Sometimes it amazes him that someone who is as "up" as Jil! usually is can also get so "down."

Rather than get Jil! mad at him again, he sits quietly, listening to the show.

The interviewer is talking to the little girl's mother, who is crying as she explains how hard it is to have a two-year-old and to run out of milk four days before she has enough money to buy more, about how hard it is to explain to the older children that they have to ration food.

"Is this some other country?" Matthew whispers to Jil!.

She shakes her head no.

Matthew thinks about the cartons of milk in his refrigerator and wishes that there were a way to mail some of them to the family.

Jil! starts to make little sniffling sounds.

Matthew puts his arm around her.

Jil! puts her head on his shoulder.

For a minute Matthew thinks about Elementary Lips but realizes that this would be really the wrong time.

Just sitting that way with Jil! makes him feel a little better, even though he still feels very bad about what is being said on television.

The interviewer is now talking to the family's doctor, who says, "When I think about poverty, it has a face. I think of this little girl and of all the people who go to bed hungry and often without shelter."

The show ends.

Matthew takes the remote control out of Jil!'s hand and turns off the television.

They just sit there quietly, staring at the television screen, even though the set has been turned off.

Kissing the hair on the top of Jil!'s head, Matthew says, "I wish we hadn't watched that."

She sighs. "Even if we hadn't watched it, she still wouldn't have enough food."

Joshua can be heard yelling out in the hall. "Okay, you guys. I'm getting ready to join you in the TV room. I'll be there in just a minute. Okay, you guys."

Loud clomping sounds can be heard in the hallway.

"I'm almost there," Joshua yells. "I'm going to count to one hundred and then I'm coming into the room."

Jil! looks at Matthew. "Exactly *what* does he think we're doing in here?"

"I told him that I was just coming in here to talk to you, to apologize." Matthew grins at her.

From the hallway Joshua can be heard. "Eighty-seven, eighty-six, eighty-five, eighty-four . . ."

Looking at each other, Jil! and Matthew start to laugh.

"Since he and Lacey have started going out," Matthew explains, "Joshua has developed a very active imagination."

"Seventy-nine, seventy-eight, seventy-seven . . ."

More sounds of clomping right outside the door can be heard.

"Should we just put him out of his misery, tell him

to come right in and start the meeting?" Jil! wipes the tears off her face and looks at Matthew.

"Sixty-five, sixty-four, sixty-three and a half . . . sixty-two . . ."

"We have a whole minute left." Matthew whispers something in Jil!'s ear.

"Sixty, fifty, forty, thirty, twenty . . . It's getting very boring waiting out here. Get ready," Joshua yells out. "Ready or not. Here I come."

As Joshua walks into the TV room, a sofa cushion held by Matthew attacks him on the left.

A sofa cushion held by Jil! hits him on the right.

Within a few seconds it is Elementary Pillow Fight.

And everyone is getting an A+.

Chapter 16

Linda Levy
"Cow"lector of Cow Things

121 Old Brompton Rd
Califon , N.J. 07830

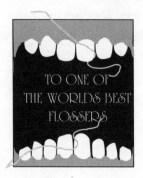

TO ONE OF
THE WORLDS BEST
FLOSSERS

SORRY THAT
YOU CAME IN
SECOND
ON

WHEEL
OF
FORTUNE

 FREE
KITTENS

Congratulations

on your

fourth marriage

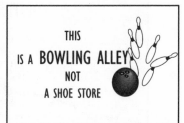

PET **WALKING**

ANIMALS-PAWS
THAT REFRESHES

CALL: PABLO MARTINEZ 908 555-7643

BRIAN BRUNO'S ROOM

KEEP OUT

(THIS MEANS _YOU_ ESPECIALLY FRITZI!!!!!!)

SORRY YOUR
FAVORITE SOAP OPERA CHARACTER
DIED

SO . . .
YOU'VE FINALLY
LEARNED TO
PROGRAM
YOUR V.C.R . . .

WELCOME HOME

IMA CARD, INK!

JIL! HUDSON
555-9763
LETTERHEADS, CARDS, SIGNS, BANNERS, MENUS
INVITATIONS

DEAR FAMILY :
☐ I LOVE CAMP.
☐ THE FOOD IS GREAT.
☐ THE FOOD IS VOMITUS.
☐ I LOVE MY BROTHER.
☐ SEND MONEY.
☐ I'M GOING TO BECOME A STAR.
☐ I PROMISE TO WRITE MORE OFTEN.
☐ I MISS MY FAMILY.
☐ I'M BEING GOOD.
☐ I'M BEING BAD.

Love,
            Amanda

CALIFON
THE BOARD GAME

"Ima Card, Ink. is doing very well," Jil! reports. "Let's go over each of these items individually so that we can learn from what we've done."

Looking at each other, Matthew and Joshua think about how they were hoping that Jil! would just split the profits three ways.

"Dr. Warren really liked his flossing cards." Jil! pastes the card into their business scrapbook. "He didn't order a lot of them because he says that there are so few good flossers in the world. I suggested that he order cards that say WORK HARD ON BEING A GOOD FLOSSER. That way he'll need a lot more cards."

Matthew raises his hand.

"It's summer. You don't have to do that," Joshua reminds him.

"I have an idea." Jumping up and down, Matthew continues to wave his hand. "How about cards that say MY FLOSSOPHY OF LIFE IS TO TAKE CARE OF MY TEETH."

Joshua groans, but says, "Good idea."

Jil! agrees, writing it down in a special notebook. "Mrs. Levy really liked her business card. And that's no bull."

Matthew just grins.

"Mr. Allen was very pleased with the card for his wife. I don't think that it's a design we'll be able to use much. After all, how many people in Califon go on *Wheel of Fortune*?" Jil! pastes the next card into the scrapbook.

"And come in second?" Matthew sticks a cupcake into his mouth.

Jil! holds up the FREE KITTENS banner. "We have to discuss this item. It seemed pretty clear to me what it meant, and we printed it the way that Mrs. Axelrod asked us to do. I don't think we should be blamed for what happened."

Matthew speaks with cupcake in his mouth. "How were we to know that Fritzi Bruno would take the kittens out of the box and set them loose around the neighborhood? That she thought that 'Free Kittens' meant 'let them loose'?"

Joshua takes a cupcake and balances it on his nose. "It's a good thing that we found them all and put them back in the box before they got hurt."

"Brian was so embarrassed." Matthew laughs, spraying cupcake crumbs. "Can you imagine having a sister like Fritzi? She probably thinks SAVE THE WHALES means putting them in a bank."

"If she lived in England," Jil!, who loves to read about royalty, adds, "and if she spelled the way that you do, Matthew, she'd probably think that it was SAVE THE WALES and decide it had something to do with the royal family."

"Just how dumb do you think I am?" Matthew pretends to pull a knife out of his heart. "How come you're always picking on me? My spelling has improved."

"Is that why you messed up Pablo's first pet-walking flier, spelling *gerbils* with an *e*?"

"There *is* an *e* in gerbils." Matthew pretends to wipe the blood off the imaginary knife.

"One *e*, not two." Jil! holds her hand out to take away the imaginary knife.

Matthew carefully hands it to her. "So no one is perfect."

Jil! locks the imaginary knife in an imaginary safe.

"You two are crazy. You two deserve each other." Joshua laughs.

Jil! continues, "That job cost us money. We had to reprint them for no extra charge. Matthew, just let me check the work before you do it. You know that's the arrangement we worked out."

"It seemed so easy and you had to spend the day baby-sitting for your little brother and helping your mother out. So I thought I could handle it myself. I showed it to him before I printed it up, so it's not totally my fault. And anyway, maybe Pablo wants to walk gerbels, not gerbils." Matthew shrugs. "Or maybe Mrs. Levy has gerBULLS for him to walk."

"I think that you've got to give in on this one," Joshua tells his best friend.

Matthew sighs, but relents. "Oh, okay."

"Now, the rest of the cards and banners went well. No problem with them," Jil! continues. "I can't believe Mrs. Arden made that VCR card for her husband because it took him four years to learn to record programs."

"My mother's never learned. No matter what station and time she puts in, she ends up recording the four A.M. show on channel seven," Joshua tells them.

"My parents were really happy with the cards we

made to send Amanda to fill in, since she's written only one letter since she's left for camp. They didn't love all of my additions but said that since we didn't charge them for that work or the stuff for Mom's store, they wouldn't charge us for the use of the machine or their supplies that we've used."

"A good deal." Jil! nods.

"And the Califon Conservancy members like our board game. They're going to sell it at Christmastime and use the money to continue to help pay off the debt for the recreation land." Jil! holds up the game. "So we didn't make a profit on it but we do have our names on the acknowledgments page."

"That's really going to help me pay for my skateboard and my big date with Lacey." Joshua makes a face.

"Where are you planning to take her? To Hawaii?" Matthew does the hula.

"There's this concert we want to go to at Garden State Center before Lacey has to go back home. My parents say we can go only if we go with my sister and her boyfriend, and my sister and her boyfriend say they'll take us only if I buy their tickets. That's four tickets." Joshua takes a bite out of a cupcake. "It's not fair, but we really want to go to the concert and Lacey doesn't want to ask her aunt for any more money."

"Bummer." Matthew licks the icing off his third cupcake.

Jil! looks into the book where she keeps track of the money. "With the way profits are going and with the jobs that we've got planned, you should have enough money for the concert in the next two weeks."

Matthew does some figuring in his head, using brain cells that he'd planned to rest over the summer vacation.

He realizes that with the money he's earning from Ima Card, Ink., the small amount of money he has managed to save from his reduced allowance, and the money he has earned from odd jobs, he should be able to buy the computer program in two weeks.

Fourteen days—and computer store . . . here comes Matthew Martin.

Chapter 17

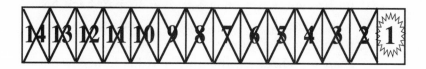

Today's the day, Matthew thinks, crossing off the last number.

Sitting on his bed, he puts the final change into coin roll packets. He counts it all up and looks on his bed at the bills, some wrinkled, some perfectly smooth, new and crisp. There are rolls of coins, all neatly sorted out—pennies, nickels, dimes, quarters—and they add up to enough money to buy the computer program, finally.

Matthew thinks about how long it took to get the

money, about how many lawns were mowed, how many errands run, about the time he sat for the Levys, and about all of the computer work that was done.

"Way to go!" Matthew says to himself, realizing that he has enough money left over to pay back his debt to his parents and his classmates and can go back to getting a normal allowance.

There's a knock on the door and his father walks into the room. "Ready, son?"

Matthew points to all of the money on the bed. "Ready. There's enough here for the program and what I owe you."

Mr. Martin smiles. "I can feel a *Leave It to Beaver* moment coming on."

Matthew thinks of all the reruns of the old shows that he has seen. "You mean one of the times when Ward Cleaver, the father, says to Beaver Cleaver, the son, 'Boy, I'm proud of you'?"

Nodding, Mr. Martin comes over and sits on the bed next to Matthew. "Yes. One of those moments."

Father and son smile at each other for a few minutes without saying a word, and then Mr. Martin speaks. "Let's make this a Martin family moment. Matthew—seriously, your mother and I are very proud of you. You worked hard. We've noticed that you're not wasting money the way you used to . . . although I have noticed that you haven't turned into a miser."

"I really needed to own this year's anthology of award-winning science fiction"—Matthew continues to smile—"even though it was kind of expensive."

"Your mother and I don't think of book buying as a luxury, but as a living expense. So that was fine, especially if you let me borrow it after you're done."

For a second Matthew thinks about charging him rent for the book but decides against it. "Sure. I'll loan it to you."

Mr. Martin ruffles his son's hair.

"Please don't do that." Matthew pats his hair back down again. "That drives me crazy. By the way, I also spent some money on junk food."

"Oh, please. Oh, please." Mr. Martin puts his hands together in a begging gesture.

"Oh, please. Oh, please, oh, what?" Matthew is very sure of what his father is going to ask for.

"Oh, please. Oh, please. Can't I ruffle your hair one more time?"

That's not what Matthew thought his father was begging for.

"And, oh, please. Oh, please. Share the junk food with your dear old dad." Mr. Martin looks like a puppy begging for a treat.

Matthew stares at his father, laughs, and lowers his head for one more hair rumpling. "Oh, okay. We have Oreos and Circus peanuts."

"Those Circus peanuts are disgusting." Mr. Martin licks his lips. "I love them."

Matthew goes over to his closet and pulls out the hidden stash of junk food, bringing it over to the bed.

As they alternate between mushing up the marshmallow Circus peanuts with their fingers and then eating them and pulling apart the Oreo cookies, eating the cream first and then the chocolate wafers, Matthew and his father collect all of the money and put it into a bag that Mr. Martin will take to the bank tomorrow.

"Are you guys ready?" Mrs. Martin calls from downstairs.

"In a minute," they yell in unison.

Matthew hides the junk food back in the closet while his father puts the cash away.

Meeting in the hall in a few minutes, they vow not to tell Mrs. Martin about their junk-food consumption.

Trying to look totally innocent, they go downstairs.

Mrs. Martin is waiting for them in the hallway.

She takes one look at their faces, which have remnants of cookie crumbs on them, and sighs.

Mr. Martin puts his arm around her waist and starts to kiss her.

She backs away and wags her finger at him. "Lips that . . ."

All three say at the same time, ". . . touch sugar will never touch mine."

Mr. and Mrs. Martin then kiss each other.

Matthew watches and says, "Is this the way to be a proper role model for your favorite son? Saying one thing and doing another?"

"Forgiveness is a good trait to learn." Mr. Martin grins.

"Did you also eat Circus peanuts?" Mrs. Martin makes a face, wiping her mouth.

Both of the Martin males hang their heads in mock shame.

"You two are impossible." Mrs. Martin looks at them. "Oh, well, let's get going."

They all pile into the family station wagon.

Matthew and Mr. Martin sing the theme songs from every television show that they remember.

By the time they get to the store, Mrs. Martin is complaining of a gigantic headache because of the singing.

Matthew and Mr. Martin know that she's kidding and sing her every aspirin commercial song that they can think of.

"I only hope that you two can behave yourselves," Mrs. Martin says as they walk into the store.

They go up to the counter.

Mr. Martin takes out his checkbook, having decided earlier not to make the sales clerk deal with all of the change and bills that Matthew has earned.

Matthew tells the sales clerk the name of the program that he wants.

The sales clerk pulls one off the shelf and tells them the price.

The program has gone on sale and is eighty dollars less than the original price.

"If only I'd known," Matthew says, "we could have already been using the program to make some of the stuff."

The salesman says, "Why don't you buy another

piece of computer equipment or another program with your savings? We have other great bargains."

Matthew looks around.

There are so many things he would like to have.

All of this extra money . . . what he earned . . . the money his parents promised him.

He looks over at the television section and sees that one of the sets is playing a rerun of the public television program that he and Jil! had seen.

He can see the same little girl, the one who has to go without milk.

Matthew turns to his parents. "Look. I want to donate the rest of the money to UNICEF, to help other kids."

"You don't want another computer program?" the sales clerk asks.

Matthew looks over at him and wants to say, *Doofus, of course I want another computer program. I just want to do this more.*

Instead he repeats, "I want to donate the money."

Both of the Martin parents smile at their son.

While Mr. Martin writes the check, Mrs. Martin comes over to Matthew and says, "Matthew, sometimes, once in a while, I can see the kind of man you are growing into—and I know that I'm going to love that grown-up very much. I want you to know how much I love the boy that you now are. I'm very proud of you."

Mr. Martin walks over, carrying the package. "And I am too."

Matthew is very happy that his parents are starting to see that he's growing up, that they are accepting that fact. He's also very happy they are in such a good mood, because there's something that he wants to discuss with them.

"Can we go to the ice-cream store and try out three of their new flavors?" He gives them his you-just-said-I'm-wonderful look, followed by the now-how-about-a-little-reward look.

"Some things never change," says Mrs. Martin with a sigh as they walk out.

"And some do." Matthew takes the package containing the computer program he has earned. "And some do."

Heading to the ice-cream store, he feels like a pioneer, going in a new direction.

"Wagons ho!" he yells.

And Matthew Martin leads the way.

About the Author

Paula Danziger is the author of a number of best-selling novels for young people, including *Remember Me to Harold Square*, *This Place Has No Atmosphere*, *It's an Aardvark-Eat-Turtle World*, *The Divorce Express*, *Can You Sue Your Parents for Malpractice?*, *There's a Bat in Bunk Five*, and *The Cat Ate My Gymsuit*.

Paula Danziger lives in New York City and Bearsville, New York. She also spends a lot of time in London.